'Tweedle,' I said.

after they threw Mouseman in jail.

'He did,' growled Mouseman, 'but now I've caught him and bent him again. I need him for a job – just as I need you two.'

'So this isn't revenge?' Blindboy said, relief in his voice. 'You're not going to kill us?'

'Not yet,' sneered Mouseman, sitting small and compact behind the wheel of the bender. 'Maybe I'll kill you afterwards. I need you to do something for me first.'

'We won't do it,' I replied, determinedly.

'Oh, yes you will,' he said softly. 'Oh, yes you will.'

Also available by Garry Kilworth
and published by Bantam:

THE ELECTRIC KID

GARRY KILWORTH

CYBER CATS

BANTAM BOOKS

TORONTO • NEW YORK • LONDON • SYDNEY • AUCKLAND

CYBERCATS
A BANTAM BOOK: 0 553 503278

First publication in Great Britain

PRINTING HISTORY
Bantam edition published 1996
Copyright © 1996 by Garry Kilworth

The right of Garry Kilworth to be identified as the author of
this work has been asserted in accordance with the Copyright,
Designs and Patents Act 1988

Condition of Sale
This book is sold subject to the condition that it shall not,
by way of trade or otherwise, be lent, re-sold, hired out or
otherwise circulated without the publisher's prior consent in any
form of binding or cover other than that in which it is published
and without a similar condition including this condition being
imposed on the subsequent purchaser.

Set in 11/14½pt Linotype Palatino by
Phoenix Typesetting, Ilkley, West Yorkshire

Bantam Books are published by Transworld Publishers Ltd,
61–63 Uxbridge Road, Ealing, London W5 5SA,
in Australia by Transworld Publishers (Australia) Pty Ltd,
15–25 Helles Avenue, Moorebank, NSW 2170,
and in New Zealand by Transworld Publishers (NZ) Ltd,
3 William Pickering Drive, Albany, Auckland.

Made and printed in Great Britain by
Cox & Wyman Ltd, Reading, Berks.

This book is for my grandson,
Jordan Lillie

1

After Blindboy and me had helped put the master criminal Mouseman in jail, we went to work for John Woo in the Golden Arcade. The arcade was situated above the covered market. There were about fifty small workshops all rented by different people. In every one of them they repaired computers, or made them up from scratch. It was a poor man's place to shop for computers and computer parts. You could have anything made up there, which had a computer at its heart.

Since Blindboy and me slept on camp beds in the shop, the arcade was our home. We ate mostly takeaway food: bamburgers and Frizzo. Junk stuff, I suppose.

Every once in a while John Woo took us out to an oriental eating house and bought us *choi sum* cabbage and green stuff like that. He kept telling us, 'You two will get scurvy if you don't eat fruit and veg. You want to get scurvy? A couple of scurvied orphans is all I need!'

We didn't know what scurvy was, but the way John Woo said it, it sounded like something really yerky. At thirteen, I'd been taught reading and writing, but Blindboy, who was two years younger than me, had never been to school. Mostly we knew what we'd learned on the streets and at the municipal dump.

'Does it bring you out in scabs and sores?' asked Blindboy. 'I hate feeling scabs on me, like when we were at the dump.'

'Your limbs fall off,' said John Woo, exaggerating as usual. 'Then your head.'

'Oh, just your head and arms and legs,' Blindboy said. 'I thought it was serious. I thought it was scabs.'

Blindboy can be just as sarcastic as anyone else, if you try to mess around with him.

The Golden Arcade was a great place, where you could hear Cantonese, Tagalog, English, Spanish, Portuguese and all kinds of languages spoken. Blindboy and me, we mostly spoke English, and a little Cantonese when we talked with John Woo.

'*Jo san*,' I would say to John Woo when he came in the morning to wake us up. '*Nie ho ma*?'

That was just saying 'Good morning, how are you?' and John Woo would usually say, '*Ho ho!*' meaning 'very good'.

Only this morning when he came in he said, '*M'ho*,' which means 'not good'.

'What's the matter, John Woo?' asked Blindboy.

We always called Mr Woo by his full name because he was an elderly gentleman, and Jack

Rickman, the cop who got us this job, told us always to be polite and respectful towards old people.

'Rubbish,' moaned John Woo. 'Streets are full of rubbish – no-one clearing it away any more. Too many mice. Too many rats. Cockroaches all over the pavement . . .'

'Doesn't impress me or Hotwire,' said Blindboy. 'We lived on the city rubbish dump, remember?'

John Woo sighed. 'Yes, but at least when it's on a dump it can be treated. Now all the dumps are getting full. There's nowhere to put rubbish any more. Trouble with the world today is, it's too crowded. There's not enough room for people *and* rubbish.

'Seven million people in this small city. Just as many in our neighbouring cities. If we go on dumping rubbish on the perimeter of town we'll be putting it in their suburbs.'

'Not enough space,' I agreed. 'They should find some way of destroying the rubbish.'

'It's difficult enough just collecting it, girl,' said John Woo. 'Let alone getting rid of it. Not enough wazzoos to carry it away. Not enough space for it when you get there. Space is the problem with this world.'

He sighed and took off his outwear coat, pulling on the old coverall he used when in the shop. It was an ancient garment covered in red and gold dragons. John Woo believed in courting good luck, with lucky colours and symbols.

'You should do some magic,' I said. 'You should make one of your dragons come to life and send it out to *eat* the rubbish in our streets.'

John Woo stopped and looked at me, strangely.

Blindboy, who obviously can't see, but can sense when something's going on, said, 'What's the silence for? Why're you two so quiet? Are we being robbed or something?'

'No,' I replied. 'John Woo is thinking.'

'You know,' said John Woo, his old wizened face looking very much like an old brown walnut when he screwed it up even further, 'you might have something there, girl. Why don't you two think about it? Some kind of machine for eating rubbish? We could put a miniature computer in it, to make it work.'

'*Ho ho*,' said Blindboy in Cantonese. 'Very good, John Woo.'

'It was me that thought of it,' I snapped at Blindboy. 'I'm the one you should say very good to.'

Blindboy smiled his blind smile. He was brilliant at hearing things, even ultrasonic sounds above the normal pitch of the human ear, while I'm good at fixing electronics.

He felt my face, to make sure I wasn't really angry.

'*You* thought of it by accident – John Woo did it on purpose.'

10

Blindboy was right, but it still made me grumpy. By that time all the other shops were opening and the technicians were getting to work, repairing computer parts, or making up boards to carry out specialist jobs inside a computer.

Everything had a microchip in it these days, from a self-heating saucepan, to a sports skidder on a race track. We always had plenty of work to do. Of course, rich people just bought new computerized goods if something went wrong with the ones they had, but there were plenty of poor people around, who needed to have their old ones repaired. Plenty. Like most cities, ours had a few thousand millionaires, then there was a big gap, going down to the people who scraped a living.

At the last count there were one million people who had no proper homes, unless you counted polythene tents on the rubbish dumps, or rail-rattler bridges as roofs over their heads, or deserted docklands. There were people who fished the polluted canals for their meals – while others, the wealthy ones, sent to far-off places for fish eggs to be flown in by fast jet for their business lunches.

Blindboy always said, 'If it's a fair world you're looking for, Hotwire, then you're on the wrong planet.'

He's always sharp, is Blindboy, and he hates to be treated like he's some kind of cripple or something.

11

'Just because I don't have any eyes,' he told people, 'doesn't mean I can't see.'

I knew what he meant, if they didn't. He had other ways of knowing what was going on around him. He wasn't stupid, like some of them wanted to treat him. John Woo said it was the dioxin in the soil that had caused so much blindness. Blindboy said he couldn't care less what it was, so long as he wasn't made to feel like some kind of freak.

Halfway through the morning I went down to the hawker stalls in the market down below and bought some egg fried rice and shanghai chicken. While we were stuffing ourselves with rice and chicken, John Woo's cat, Citizen Kane, came out from under some polystyrene packing cases where he had been sleeping. He was drawn of course by the smell of the food and made a fuss until we gave him some. He scoffed it down quickly.

'Hey,' I said, staring at Citizen Kane, 'that's what we should do – we should make a cat eat the rubbish! That way we wouldn't upset ordinary people. That way you get rid of the rubbish where it is, and don't have to carry it to the city limits. I mean, if you put something like a dragon on the streets, they're bound to get jumpy aren't they – they'll say it's spooky. But a cat?'

'One cat wouldn't be any good,' pointed out Blindboy, deftly eating rice with his chopsticks. 'You'd need a lot.'

'So we make a lot,' I said. 'I bet the town council would pay us to do it, if we came up with a – a – protty—'

'A prototype,' finished John Woo for me.

'Yes, one of those things,' I said, nodding.

'Let's do one, then,' cried Blindboy. 'I'm fed up with talking about it. Let's do one.'

John Woo came forward with some practical problems.

'What are you going to use for the skins? I presume you want it to look like a real cat? You can't go around skinning alley cats – people wouldn't like it.'

'How can you say such a thing?' I cried, not seeing the joke. 'That's terrible.'

'Yes it is, so how are you going to do it?' he insisted.

Blindboy said, 'Hey, what about the false fur place, down the road?'

'Synthetic Furs Ltd?' said John Woo. 'They might do it for you – at a price.'

'Well, we could afford *one* cat skin, couldn't we? Then if the council want some more, they'll have to pay for them.'

John Woo nodded. 'That sounds a good plan. But I've got a second problem now. If these cats of yours eat all the rubbish, what happens to it inside them? I mean, there has to be some waste, even if you eat it.'

I said, 'I've already thought of that. I went to

school once and they told us matter exists in three states . . .'

'What does?' asked Blindboy.

'Matter, stuff, you know, *anything*. Well then, you can turn a liquid into a solid by freezing it, can't you? Or a liquid into a gas by boiling it to steam or whatever. Well, we can turn trash into gas and just let it blow away.'

'Smelly gas?' Blindboy said, wrinkling his nose.

'Doesn't have to smell,' I told him. 'At least, it doesn't have to smell *bad*. Some gases don't. Some gases don't smell at all. We could have an – an—'

'An *odourless* gas?' suggested John Woo.

'That's it – one of those,' I said. 'We could turn all the rubbish into a harmless, odourless gas that just blows away.'

I stared at the pair of them, the old man with his thoughtful face, and the boy with his thoughtful face, and hoped they weren't thinking up new problems between them. This is the trouble with being a genius like me; people always try to knock you off your perch, like a cocky parrot. I'm always coming up with brilliant ideas, only to have Blindboy or John Woo chuck problems in the way. They always look so smiffing smug about it too. It makes me so mad sometimes.

Blindboy said nothing.

John Woo eventually turned his face to me and spoke. 'An electro-mechanical rubbish-eating cat,' he said. 'That's brilliant, Hotwire. You're a genius.'

Blindboy smiled at this, turning his shining face towards the dirty window where the sun was lighting up the cobwebs, making them glint with rainbow colours.

I stared at the pair of them suspiciously.

'Are you making a kerk out of me?' I said.

'Would we do that?' asked Blindboy, still smiling. 'A brilliant genius like you? Would we?'

'You might,' I said.

'O, ye of little faith!' John Woo exclaimed. 'Hotwire, you have to learn to take a bit of kidding. Here, take this money and go to the false fur factory – ask them if they can make up a cat fur to look like the real thing. Blindboy, you get that brain of yours into gear and start thinking of a chip to go in the cat. I'm going to get a cd on science – we need to find out how to turn rubbish into odourless, harmless gas.'

'Is that all I get to do?' I complained. 'Buy the yerky cat skin?'

'You, young lady, have to make the mechanical parts that eat the rubbish, with those delicate hands you have there.'

I looked down at my calloused palms and fingers, then realized he was kidding again.

'Don't call me "young lady",' I said. 'That isn't even kidding – that's not a joke – it's blasphemy.'

They both laughed.

15

I hitched up my oversized overalls, rolled the legs up to the knees so that they wouldn't trip me up, then I ran down the stairs to the rest of the market below and into the street, barging my way through the crowd. The trouble with the city today is that there's too many people. Too many people in the world, if you ask me, though I haven't been outside this one city yet. I'm told nowhere else is any different.

Now I had rubbish to battle through as well as people, because the stuff was piled on every street corner. There were mountains of it, contained in big vegie bags that had been ripped open by rats, cats, dogs and foxes, to spill their innards. Cabbage stalks, magazines, cardboard boxes, biodegradable containers, dinner sludge, breakfast slime, lunch muck, and so on. The cockroaches were having a party with it, especially since these days there was little plastic around.

The alleys were full of the stuff too, so you couldn't get past it, and had to go a long way around.

Rubbish and people. Every day you hear about millions of people dying of famine, or disease, or just plain old war, and it doesn't seem to make sense. Yet there it is, millions of people being born every day, millions of people dying, and still the world is crowded shoulder to shoulder with people.

I saw a cop I knew, sitting in a parked bender.

'Hey, Dave, how's it with you?' I yelled.

'Familiar kid,' he grimaced.

'My pal Sergeant Jack Rickman doesn't think I'm familiar,' I said, 'so there's no need to get yerky on me.'

He stopped sipping his hot coffee and said in a smug voice, 'Your *pal* Jack has been seconded to another city for a while – when he gets back he won't even know you.'

I stopped, dumbfounded. 'What's seconded mean?'

'It means,' said the cop's partner, 'that Rickman won't be around for a while. He's been sent to solve some case up north – something to do with Mouseman.'

'Mouseman's in jail,' I said. 'Blindboy and me put him there, see.'

'Yes, but part of his empire is still operating, kid, and since Rickman knows all about Mouseman, since he's the *big cheese* where Mouseman is concerned – hey, get the joke? – anyway, he's the man on the job. His partner Phil's gone with him. So don't get too cocky, you little kerk, or we'll throw you in the sweatshops for a few days while your *pal* Sergeant Rickman is away out of reach. You get me, girl?'

'Huh!' I grumbled. 'All that, just because I said hello. Next time, I'll ignore you.'

'You do that. Now move along, kid.'

The other one called after me, 'When are you

going to start wearing dresses, girl? You look a mess.'

'I'll wear a frock when you do a full day's work,' I yelled back, 'which means *never*.'

Some cops are like that. They think they own the street. They sit there drinking coffee and lazing around while all the criminals in the world have a holiday. Jack wasn't like that. Jack was always on the ball. And he didn't need to roust street kids to get his kicks. That's what I liked about him. Him and his wife Barb were good people.

I arrived at the false fur factory and went inside.

2

The fur people said yeah, they could supply me with stuff that looked like cat's skin. I bought some of it and then walked back to the Golden Arcade. The cops had gone when I passed the spot where they had been waiting. It gave me a funny feeling to think that Jack Rickman was no longer in the city. I sort of thought of him as someone to run to in times of trouble, and now he wasn't there it worried me a little.

When you looked down the streets around the arcade, packed with markets of all kinds, selling anything from needles to flagpoles, it was full of kerks and slummers. There were yerky types on every corner, waiting to make a deal on something not-quite-legal, or plain illegal. Anything to make a dollar. They would sell the rubbish, if they could've found someone to buy it, just to make a few bucks.

Behind the shutters in many buildings the rooms seethed with card schools and other gambling games. In these rooms money exchanged hands in great quantities. Drug deals went on too, behind thick curtains, thin walls and boxwood

19

doors. That was the really scary thing about this city, the drugs and stuff.

I'm told dope trafficking goes on in all cities. But when you see the junkies drooling their way to death or to becoming mindless cabbages, and then you see the fat wallets of the dealers who prey on them, you wonder whether God dished out brains in teaspoons to some people. Dope is the right word for it: dopes pay lots of money to dig themselves a nasty little grave.

I got back to the arcade, which is on two levels, with us on the first floor.

'Did you get it?' asked Blindboy, recognizing my step. 'Do we go to work?'

'I got it,' I confirmed. 'Here, feel it.'

I handed it over to my best friend, who rubbed the synthetic fur against his cheek.

'Doesn't feel much like moggie fur,' he said, 'but I guess it's OK so long as it looks like it. What is it, tabby or ginger?'

'This one's going to be a black cat, but they'll give us the other shades when we want more.'

'Good,' said John Woo, returning after dealing with a customer who had come for a joystick board. 'Let's get to work.'

We studied the cd on science, filling ourselves with all sorts of knowledge. Having computers around is swazz for that sort of thing. You can get information programs on anything these days, from building your own skidder or bender, to finding out what kind of insect is crawling on your collar.

I began work on the mechanics of the thing, while John Woo and Blindboy worked on the chip.

Blindboy had a Braille computer keyboard, which helped him with the software. When he printed a hard copy, it too was in Braille, but mostly he worked with a vocal soundboxed computer. He gave it spoken instructions and it answered him in one of those spooky computer voices, telling him what he wanted to know.

In this way he didn't need any help from us. Blindboy hated to fuss over his lack of sight. He was a pretty independent person, when it came to things like that.

I used to worry a bit, about what went on inside Blindboy, because he could get very angry at times. Especially he hated strangers going all gooey over him, slipping money into his hand and saying things like, 'Oh, you poor boy.'

Blindboy would drop the money on the floor. 'I'm not poor,' he would growl. 'I'm as rich as Croesus, see. Don't you call me poor.'

One day I said to him, 'Blindboy, you're telling whoppers – you're not rich at all, not like that ancient king or whatever you keep talking about.'

'Croesus,' Blindboy replied, 'was the king of a country called Lydia, in Asia Minor. Around 500 BC he had more money than any other person in the world. He had buckets full of gold and diamonds and stuff. I learned all that in a history cd.'

'But you're not rich,' I said.

'Nor is Croesus, *now*,' grinned Blindboy. 'He's *dead*.'

You had to give Blindboy his due, he could talk his way around a roadblock.

Well, without going into boring detail, though John Woo loved to talk to his fellow shop-owners for hours about it over endless cups of *bo lei* tea, we made the first electro-mechanical cat. In the bad light of an alley, at night, it would look as real as any mouser, be it tom or queen. I was dead proud of it. It was as swazz as any moggie I had ever seen.

'What shall we call her?' I asked.

'You mean *him*, don't you?' said Blindboy.

John Woo intervened, before an argument broke out between us kids. 'Why not give it a name that hasn't got a gender?'

'What does that mean?' I asked, suspiciously. After all, John Woo was a male too, even if he was old.

'A name which could be either boy or girl,' replied John Woo. 'Can I suggest one?'

'All right,' we said together.

From the man who named his own cat Citizen Kane, we expected something exotic.

'How about *Chip*? The connection is obvious.'

'Boy's name,' I cried. 'I knew it – it's a con-spiracy.'

'All right, what about *Mac*, for Mechanical Automated Cat?'

'Another boy's name.'

'Right, here's one that can be either – *Cybercat*?'

'Yes!' I cried.

Blindboy replied, 'All right by me.'

'That's it then, Cybercat One.'

We gave Cybercat a stale cake to eat and it gob-bled it down in two seconds flat, the mechanical jaws snapping quickly. Within less time the cake was turned into gas by the electro-chemical stom-ach of our invention and released into the air through thousands of tiny holes in the cat's skin.

Blindboy had suggested we let the gas come out of its backside, but I thought that was gross. We had to sell this idea to a lot of a stuffy councillors. To present them with a farting moggie, no matter *how* odourless the gases, would be to pronounce a death sentence on our plan.

'A natural idea,' John Woo told Blindboy, 'but I think Hotwire's right, under the circumstances.'

'The next experiment,' I said, 'is to take Cyber-cat down to the rubbish dump.'

'Yeah,' smiled Blindboy. 'We could see all our pals!'

John Woo found us an old cat-carrier and we put our electro-mechanical cat in this to lug around like a pet.

We went down to the hubbub in the streets below, where the crowds milled and mashed each other's toes. It took quite a while to reach the dump, since we had to climb or go around mountains of rubbish to get there. Some of the piles of garbage had reached as high as the gutters on a two-storey building. Blindboy said it was as if the world had been created again, by a god who wanted a lot more hills and valleys, a lot more pongy smells, and was keen on breeding cockroaches and rats.

Blindboy can get quite poetical at times.

The dump was on the outskirts of the city on a raised plateau of rubbish. When we lived there, under polythene tents, we could look down on the swazz rash of city lights at night, as they crackled and fizzed out their colours. It had been the best thing about the dump; the worst being the diseases you could catch, and the filthy food you had to eat.

The garbage wazzoos were bringing their loads of rubbish by the hour, but they were fighting a losing battle.

'Hey, Buzzard!' I yelled to a dump kid I knew. Then to another, 'Hey, Oilslick!'

There was a bit of a reunion with the other dump kids, who'd not yet managed to escape like we had. They had their tales to tell, we had ours. Once these were out of the way, we explained to them why we had come to the dump.

24

'Let's see it work, then,' said Oilslick.

We put the cybercat down on the dump floor and switched it on. It began eating straightaway, munching its way through the rubbish. Every so often it stopped, hissed out gas, and then went back to work again.

'Would you look at that?' cried Freezer, another kid. 'It's going to eat us out of a home.'

All the kids laughed at this. The only reason they lived on the dump was to get at the garbage early, to find things that might be useful, things they could fix up and sell.

'It's not for up here,' Blindboy told them. 'It's for the streets, to get rid of all the edible stuff. You'll still get all the old fridges and stereos, only you won't have to sort through muck to get at them . . .'

While he was talking, a garbage man arrived with a wazzoo and began unloading. He saw the cybercat, munching away quite near him, so being a kerk he picked up a rock and threw it. It struck our cat on the back.

'Take that, you mangy tom,' he said, laughing.

'Hey!' I yelled. 'That's our cat, mister.'

He threw a second missile, this time an empty bottle.

'That's what I think of your cat, you slummer. Get it off my dump.'

This time the missile hit the cat directly on the head and it suddenly whirled and raced around in circles, as if chasing its own tail.

'You kerk,' I shouted. 'You've damaged it.'

'*Injured* it, you mean,' said the dump man, looking in amazement as the cat flew around at a fantastic speed. 'It's gone crazy.'

Suddenly the cat did two perfect somersaults in the air, then landed on its feet. It was pointing directly at the garbage man. It rushed forwards, its jaws snapping like a land piranha, as if looking for something to chomp.

'Wha . . . !' cried the garbage man. 'Get it off!'

The trouble was, the garbage man had on these vegie trousers, the kind you throw away after a day's work. They were made of some kind of fibre woven from coconut trees. You could soil them as much as you liked and it saved washing. They went into the pigswill with the rest of the edible muck.

Our ravenous cat, who was never anything but starving, went straight for this source of food.

Before the man had a chance to run, our cat had eaten up to his underpants, and was still nibbling swiftly.

'Get it off! Get it off!' he shrieked, trying to swat the cat, which managed to dodge every blow.

'Hey,' laughed Freezer, 'that cat's got rabies, mister – you ought to go and get some injections after this.'

When the cat had eaten all his trousers, it dropped to the ground and raced smack inside an empty oil drum. We heard it hit the end with a loud booming note. A bulge appeared in the bottom of the drum, made by the cat's plastimetal head. The cybercat then staggered out. Its tail spun on its bottom several times, then it flopped over and lay twitching on the ground.

Finally, it hissed gases like a steam engine from every pore, then lay perfectly still.

'There was two dollars in my pocket,' yelled the garbage man. 'It ate my two dollars.'

He was trying to hide his knobbly legs with a piece of sheet metal he had found, since he was now wearing nothing but his red polka-dot underpants behind it.

'That cat was worth more than two dollars, you yerky kerk,' Blindboy yelled back. 'We ought to charge you for it.'

The man's expression changed. He dropped his sheet metal plate and came running forwards, roaring as he did so.

The kids scattered over the dump, heading for all their favourite hiding places. I grabbed Blindboy's hand and we ran too. With my other hand I snatched up the broken cybercat as we ran past it.

We headed down the sloping cliff of earth and rubbish to the dirt track down below. Cans and bottles began to land around us as we rushed away from the scene. The garbage man was hurling things at us. Soon we were out of range and I turned and yelled something more at him, then we hit the streets.

27

Back at the Golden Arcade, we told John Woo what had happened.

'The cybercat worked, then, until the garbage man threw a rock at it?'

'It was the bottle that did the damage – yeah, it worked a treat,' I said. 'It was woofing down rubbish like nobody's business.'

John Woo took the limp form from my hands. 'Right,' he said, 'let's perform a resurrection and then arrange a date to see the city elders, eh?'

We soon got Cybercat up and working again. And through some influential friends, John Woo got us a meeting with the city council. We put Cybercat in his carrier again and went to the house on the hill, where the councillors sat in judgement on our daily lives. I wore my best overalls.

Since we had saved the city from Mouseman there had been an election and a new council controlled the city. These people didn't know us, as the whole business of Mouseman planting bombs and being caught by a couple of kids had been kept a secret. The police had advised the last mayor against alarming the people of the city. John Woo said no-one wanted to tell the world a large city had been saved by two kids, either.

Blindboy and me had been heroes, but only to the last mayor and a few cops.

'What's the matter with the little boy?' asked the new mayor, when the three of us stood before a long false-mahogany desk that gleamed like real wood.

28

Blindboy turned and peered over his own shoulder, as if looking for the kid in question.

'What little boy?'

'You,' answered a fat councillor sitting behind the desk. 'She's talking about you, boy.'

'Nothing wrong with me,' replied Blindboy, staring directly at the voice he had heard. 'Anything wrong with you?'

There was silence for a while, during which the mayor stared at Blindboy, then, when the fat man was about to speak again, she waved a hand at him to stop him.

'Let's proceed,' she said. 'I understand you have an answer to our rubbish problem? What is it?'

'Cybercats!' I said, holding up our prototype.

The woman raised her eyebrows, which I noticed had been tattooed on her forehead. There's not much in this world of ours that isn't false in some way.

'Cy-ber-cats,' she repeated, slowly.

A woman on the panel snorted, derisively, but the mayor held up her hand again.

'How does it work?' she asked, signalling a security man in the corner.

I glanced at the burly security man nervously as he ambled towards the front of the desk.

'It eats the rubbish,' I said. 'You need a lot of them to make it work properly.'

'What happens to the waste?' said the fat man.

'Comes out as harmless, odourless gas,' answered Blindboy.

'Harmless and odourless?' repeated another man.

'Absolutely,' confirmed John Woo.

'You know,' said a councillor in glasses with a silver chain attached to them in a loop behind his head, 'that salt, for example, is made up of the chemicals sodium and chloride. Chlorine gas is very poisonous. What I'm asking is, what happens if there's some salt in the rubbish, and you've got robot cats wandering around, passing wind and killing everyone.'

'Don't be vulgar, Arthur,' said the woman. 'Joe,' she snapped at the security man, 'would you get us a bag of rubbish?'

Joe looked at her astonished. 'Ma'am?'

'You heard what the mayor said,' Arthur muttered, 'get us a bag full of garbage.'

The security man went out, shaking his head. I let out a sigh of relief, having thought the mayor was going to tell him to throw us out onto the street. The security man returned with a large vegie bag full of garbage.

'Tip it out on the floor,' ordered the mayor.

'Yes, ma'am,' answered the security man, knowing better than to question her again.

He poured the contents of the bag onto the shiny floor of the council chamber. There were vegie coffee cups, food slops, one or two metal cans, lots of waste paper, string and various other sorts of trash. I put our cat down and it went straight for the rubbish and started eating it, going ten to the dozen. In a few minutes all the rubbish was gone except the two cans, which the cybercat licked clean.

'Brilliant,' said the mayor, raising her tattooed eyebrows. 'What about the gas?'

'It's been releasing the gas slowly, while it's been eating.'

The councillors looked at each other, as if surprised they hadn't smelled anything or keeled over dead.

The mayor asked, 'And the cans?'

'It won't eat metal, but ninety-five per cent of the rubbish is edible,' said John Woo. 'The garbage wazzoos can pick up the metal things.'

'And when people see this – this *creature* in the streets at night, they'll just take it for an ordinary alley cat?' said the mayor.

'That's the idea, lady,' replied Blindboy. 'You just give us the money and we'll make a thousand cybercats for you. There's dozens of shops like ours in the Golden Arcade – they're all looking for work. We'll clear the streets in no time.'

'You've got it,' said the mayor. 'Get to work.'

3

When we got back from the council chamber, we went round the other shops and recruited workers to make cybercats. The other technicians were just as keen as we were to do the job. It felt as if we were working for the government on a secret project, which I suppose is what we were doing.

The fur factory was happy to have a big order, too.

After a few weeks, we had five thousand cats out on the streets, chomping away at the rubbish, reducing the piles. We had programmed them to work only at night. When the dawn came up, which, because of the pollution, was usually a cruel yellow colour, the cybercats would sneak away. They went off to hide in the nuclear shelters below the council offices. In the event of a war, the mayor said, the cats would be instantly evicted.

There was one problem we hadn't anticipated.

The *real* cats, and the dogs.

One night, soon after we'd put the cybercats onto the street, Blindboy and me went out to see how they were getting on. It was a hot, humid evening. You couldn't see the stars, because of the lights of the city, and anyway the sky had this hazy layer between us and the heavens all the time, even at night. The haze and the yellow dawns were all due to the bad air.

There were plenty of night creasers out in the city streets, conning the citizens out of their money, or just plain robbing them. Cops on motorzips were in short supply, fighting a losing battle over law and order.

There were street urchins by the dozen, running up and down side roads, grabbing a crust where they could.

Two more brats in the crowd didn't attract attention from the overworked cops.

'I love the night-time streets,' Blindboy said, as we fought against the mass of bodies. 'You can smell all the hawker stalls – the satays and the noodles. It's real swazz, Hotwire.'

I was busy watching the creasers, watching us watching them. They stared with narrowed eyes at Blindboy and me. I knew what some of them were thinking: here's a couple of kids we can put to work.

Kids like us were used to send crawling through small windows. Or to push up over high fences that adults were too scared to climb. Or to force down sewer pipes.

We were made to open doors from the inside so that creasers could get into buildings and rob the rich. Not to give to the poor though, unless you include the creasers themselves in that group.

Being sightless, Blindboy was not aware of this undercurrent of sinister stares. He just heard the feet on the pavements and smelled the hawker stalls. He just felt the wind of the skidders and benders going past, felt the vibrations from the underground rail rattlers. Occasionally the roar of a motorzip weaving through the wazzoos had him cocking his head in the direction of the traffic. But he didn't sense the stares.

When we came to an alley, we wandered down, to see our cybercats at work.

The first thing we witnessed was real cats leaping on our cybercats and ripping fur from their backs in chunks. There was a territorial war going on. A dog pack had cornered another of them and the mutts were using their jaws to toss it to each other like a rag doll. It was mayhem. At the end of the alley, two bag ladies were beating one of our cybercats with bin lids.

'Hey, ladies,' I called. 'Why're you hurting that cat?'

They paused for a moment, allowing the cybercat to trundle away on three good legs, its tail spinning.

'It ate our bags up,' yelled one of the women.

The other added, 'And everythin' in 'em!'

There was worse to come.

We met drunks who were trying to kick our cats

along the gutter, and tramps who caught them and used them for pillows.

'It's terrible out there,' we complained to John Woo. 'Everyone is attacking our project.'

John Woo said, 'Well, we can make them aggressive towards other cats and against dogs, rats and foxes – that ought to keep the animal life at bay. But we can't make them hostile towards people. You can't have machines going round biting bag ladies and tramp men on the ankles, can you?'

'Why not?' asked Blindboy, but he didn't mean it. He was just miffed that the project was going wrong. 'Tell you what we can do,' he added. 'We can make 'em *fast*.'

'Yes,' I said. 'Make 'em so they can't be caught.'

So that's what we did: we rounded them all up and repaired the damaged ones. Then we programmed them to be hostile towards feral cats and other four-legged attackers. We used laser beams for their eyes. Every so often the cybercat would turn its head and scan the area around it for real beasts.

Any furry or hairy creature giving out body heat that was less than a metre away and of a certain size, would cause a reaction in the cybercat. The cybercat would face the creature, its hair would stand on end, it would arch its back and spit. In fact it would act just like a real cat. If the live creature came any closer, the cybercat would make short rushes at it, threatening to fight to the bitter end.

'On reflection,' said John Woo, 'we can't have the cybercats biting any small humans. I don't suppose there's any aggressive five-year-old kids wandering the alleys wearing fur coats, but you can't take chances on things like that.'

Blindboy also programmed the cybercats to avoid larger creatures, giving them the speed to escape human beings, big dogs and wild grizzly bears. Blindboy said he had never heard of grizzly bears being seen in the city, but you couldn't take chances on things like that.

I suppose he was kidding, but you never could tell with Blindboy, because he said it so seriously.

We put the cybercats back out on the streets again, and this time it worked fine. When we checked the alleys at night our cats were eating the rubbish with gusto, sharing the territory with real cats, and dogs, rats and foxes. In fact, our cats ate up the rubbish that was left by the real creatures, who couldn't stomach paper, cardboard or cabbage stalks.

The rubbish began to disappear and the council were delighted.

With the extra income John Woo received from the council for all this we took out another shop on the ground floor. These shops were more expensive than the first floor shops, being amongst the food and clothing stalls, but more customers went past. There was more chance of buyers down there.

John Woo took three more kids off the dump. They had to be kids that were good with computers, kids that could be trusted with money, and kids that actually *wanted* to work in the Golden Arcade.

Zazz, Muffler and Oilslick were those kids.

Zazz and Oilslick were boys and Muffler was a girl. Muffler used to share a tent on the dump with Sofa, a little fat girl, but Sofa died after eating something that had rat poison on it.

Muffler was very clever with software. She had once had her own computer, bought for her by her foster parents. Those same foster parents were now in jail for computer fraud. Muffler had run away to the dump, rather than go in a home for children of prisoners of the state. No other family had wanted her, being nearly twelve years of age.

Zazz was like me, good at hardware, only not so brilliant. Not a genius like me.

Oilslick was a mouth, good at selling. He could talk you into buying his grandmother. Most people didn't even know what they were acquiring from Oilslick until they walked away with it and looked down at what they were carrying in their hands.

One day, I was passing under the newsscreen in the main square of the city when I looked up and saw something that made my heart do a flip-flop.

37

The newscreen said: INFAMOUS CONVICTS ESCAPE. MOUSEMAN, THE MAD BOMBER, AND HIS ACCOMPLICE ALPHONSE GROTE ESCAPED THIS MORNING FROM STATE PRISON.

The master criminal I had put behind bars was out of jail and no doubt looking for revenge.

I stared around me, quickly scanning the faces of the crowd, expecting at any moment to see a squat man in a tight sharp suit staring at me with glinting little eyes.

I didn't know who Alphonse Grote was, but I didn't like the sound of his name. Mouseman was well-known for choosing hard men with no brains for his accomplices. In that way he kept all the power for himself and had someone to do the dirty work.

I hurried back to the Golden Arcade.

Blindboy had already heard the news, on the speakers, and was ready for me.

'*He's* escaped,' he said.

'I know,' I replied.

For a moment neither of us could think of anything to say. When our brains thawed from the fear, I said hopefully, 'Maybe he'll go to another city – or even another country? Maybe he won't even remember us?'

'Fat chance,' said Blindboy. 'I bet he's been lying in a ratty, cockroachy cell pulling the legs off helpless spiders and wishing they were us.'

I sighed. 'I bet you're right, too. I bet his brain has been simmering like a steaming pot of noodles with thoughts of death and destruction. I bet that top of the list of things he wants to do now is a note to remind himself to murder us.'

'No doubt about it,' Blindboy replied, refusing to offer himself or me any shred of comfort.

Jack Rickman was still out of town, and his partner Phil was with him. We really didn't trust any other cops. Jack and his wife Barb were like family to us. We didn't see them often, but when we did they fussed over us. They couldn't look after us in their tiny apartment, but we wouldn't have wanted that anyway. Blindboy and me had been independent for too long.

'We could run away,' I said.

Blindboy asked, 'To another planet?'

'Yeah,' I replied, sighing, 'we'd have to go that far to get away from Mouseman, wouldn't we? At least he hasn't got Gorilla Joe and Kevin A with him this time.'

'No, but he's got some guy called *Grote*. Can you imagine what a guy called Grote is going to look like?'

'Big,' I said.

'Very big.'

John Woo was sympathetic of course. 'I'm not going to let anyone march in here and take you away – neither will any of the other technicians around here. You'll just have to stay off the streets until he's caught, that's all. Lay low, kids. If he's in this city, they'll catch him.'

So that's what we did, we kept our heads down.

A couple of weeks went by and there was still no news about Mouseman. I was beginning to get cabin fever. Then a big robbery took place. Someone tunnelled into the main city bank and cut their way into the vault. Two million dollars was stolen. Blindboy and me knew exactly who had done it.

'Mouseman,' I said.

'And Grote,' he added.

Two million dollars was just pocket change to Mouseman. He probably needed that much to set himself up again, with a secure hideout from which to operate. A bank robbery was a crude act for a criminal like Mouseman. He actually specialized in holding cities to ransom and demanding *hundreds* of millions of dollars. The bank job was just stake money, with which he would purchase chemicals to poison the water system, or bomb-making equipment, or cylinders of noxious gases.

'We're doomed,' I groaned.

'Doomed,' agreed Blindboy.

In the meantime, our cybercats were working well, clearing the streets of rubbish as we planned.

John Woo explained our problem to the council, but they weren't interested. Money was short, there were many corrupt officials, and kids on the streets were simply nothing more than a nuisance. The mayor seemed honest enough but when she was approached by John Woo, she asked what could she do?

To give us protection she would have had to take cops off the streets. There were already too few of them. She suggested that we put ourselves in the hands of the prison officials. They could keep us in jail for a while, out of harm's way, but Blindboy and me had a horror of city jails. You could get forgotten. We might never get out again.

'Can't you just ask the police to watch the Golden Arcade?' suggested John.

'They're already doing that,' replied the mayor, 'in between watching every other building and establishment in the city. You don't seem to realize, we're overcrowded and chronically underfunded. We have the homeless, the helpless and the desperate to look after in their thousands. It's impossible. The whole thing is a mess. I've got more on my plate than two orphans scared of bogeymen.'

'I understand your problems,' John Woo said, 'I live in amongst the mess, too. But these are no bogeymen – they're real, live, escaped convicts.'

'Have the kids been attacked?' she asked.

'No, not yet – but . . .'

'Come and see me if or when this Mouseman tries to get at them.'

'It might be too late then,' John Woo complained.

The mayor shook her head. 'I personally don't

41

think anything will come of this. Mouseman and Grote are probably hiding in some foreign country. I don't think we'll hear from them again this century.'

'What about the robbery? The kids are sure it was them.'

'If it was, Mouseman probably bought airline tickets with the money, believe me.'

And that was that. No help from that quarter.

We just had to sweat it out.

4

When we read about how Mouseman and Grote escaped from prison, it was pretty clever. Some computer freak on the outside hacked into the jail's computer network. Once this someone was hooked into the security system, they opened the door to Mouseman and Grote's cell. This allowed the pair to slip out into the main thoroughfare of the prison.

The escaping duo knew that the prison officers were having a fancy dress party in the dining hall that night. They opened a back window to the dining hall toilets and climbed inside, waiting in one of the cubicles. During the evening, officers came and went, until finally two officers came in, one dressed as a giant panda, the other as a wizard.

Before the two officers knew what was happening, Mouseman and Grote had grabbed them, gagged them and tied them up. They took the costumes, Grote forcing himself into the giant panda suit, and Mouseman putting on the wizard's clothes.

Because Mouseman's suit had no mask to it and his face could be seen, he pretended to be drunk.

Grote draped Mouseman over his shoulder, with his face hidden against his back, and then went out of the toilets and into the party.

'What's the matter with him?' an officer dressed as a highwayman cried.

'Too much to drink,' muttered Grote. 'Taking him home.'

The officer frowned and said, 'Your voice sounds a bit funny.'

'It's this suit,' Grote grumbled. 'It muffles me.'

Grote then started walking out of the main door to the hall, when a woman called from the far side of the hall, 'Where are you going?'

This was obviously the wife of one of the two prison officers locked in the toilet cubicle.

'Home,' growled Grote. He swung the limp Mouseman around. 'Drunk.'

'Well, me and Sue are staying, aren't we Sue?'

A woman next to her nodded. 'We're not coming home yet,' she complained. 'We're having a nice time. You can come back and fetch us at midnight.'

'Right,' growled Grote. 'Midnight.'

Then Grote simply walked out into the night, across the courtyard, towards the main gates. The officer in the guardhouse asked to see their identification cards. Grote produced the two cards, taken from their owners. The guard took them and flashed them over a computer scanner.

The scanner said it did not recognize the cards

as belonging to the two people standing in front of it.

'*Not compatible!*' it had stated, loudly.

Grote and Mouseman must have thought they were done for at that point, but the guard then said, 'It's the fancy dress costumes – the security computer doesn't recognize you in them. You remember we had the same trouble with officers on their way *in* tonight.'

'Oh, right,' growled Grote, 'I remember.'

Once the pair were outside the prison gates they shed their costumes and fled into the night.

'So that's how they escaped?' said Blindboy.

'That's it,' I confirmed. 'You've got to hand it to Mouseman, he's no kerk.'

'He *is* a kerk,' Blindboy argued, 'otherwise he wouldn't have been in jail in the first place, Hotwire.'

John Woo said, 'You two had better stay off the streets until that fiend is caught. You'll be safe enough here, but don't go out of the Golden Arcade.'

'How are we going to eat?' I complained. 'We need our Frizzo and bamburgers.'

'*Sai gwa tau!*' John Woo said, calling me a 'watermelon head'. 'Hotwire, Blindboy, I will make sure you get fed. If you go outside you might not have anything to eat with.'

I felt my throat, realizing John Woo was right.

'I wish Jack Rickman and Barb were here,' I complained. 'I'd feel safer with them around.'

'I am your family,' John Woo said, sternly. 'We Chinese look after our own family.'

I looked at the old man and had trouble not bursting into tears. He had said he was our family! Since my dad had died I always wanted to be part of a family. I had Blindboy, who was like a brother to me, but that didn't seem quite enough to make a whole family. When Barb and Jack had us stay with them at one time, I thought they might be my family.

Now this old Chinese gentleman had said he was my family and it was true.

He had taken us in, given us a roof over our heads, given us a job to do. He had made us proud of ourselves.

'Are you our grandfather now?' I asked.

John Woo smiled and his face creased like an old, worn map. 'I'm only seventy-two years old,' he said, 'but I think I'm probably ready to be a *lo naam yan*.'

'Does that mean yes?' asked Blindboy.

'If you want it to,' replied John Woo, 'but you have to know what you're taking on. In a Chinese family old people are respected. Grandfathers are very important – the older they get the more important they become. You have to be *twice* as respectful to grandmothers, only we haven't got one of those, so you don't need to worry. You have to treat older family members with the utmost care and attention, listen to what they say, take advice from them because they have wisdom, never laugh at them for being old and silly, even when they *are* old and silly. They have lived longer, have more experience of life.'

'Sounds swazz to me,' I said. 'What do we call you?'

'You call me John Woo like always,' answered our new grandfather, firmly. 'I don't want all my friends here thinking I'm ancient. *Grandfather* sounds prehistoric.'

'But how will they know we're family?' I protested, disappointed.

John Woo shook his head slowly and smiled again. 'They already know that – they know I adopted you two the day you came here.'

So we did as our grandfather told us, and stayed in the market. While we were surrounded by many friends in the Golden Arcade, which was like one *big* family, all looking after each other, Mouseman couldn't get at us. It was only if we went out on to the streets we would be in trouble. All we had to do was stay inside four wide walls until Mouseman was caught.

One day Blindboy and me were pretty fed up with being in the shop, looking at the same scene hour after hour.

'Let's go downstairs, into the market,' I said. 'John Woo won't be back until midday.'

'Aren't we supposed to stay here?' asked Blindboy.

'Well, yeah, in the building,' I replied, 'but the market downstairs is in the building, isn't it?'

Blindboy nodded. 'I suppose so.'

'Let's get an iced lime juice from Celery Chang's hawker stall,' I suggested. 'It's a really hot day.'

'OK,' shrugged Blindboy.

We locked up the grid on the front of the shop and went down the rattling escalator to the market below. It was thick with people down there, all buying snakes, chickens, *choi sum* cabbage, crabs, frogs, bananas, watercress, and all kinds of food. The floor was slippery and slimy where the stall owners had washed fish and thrown the water into the gutter channels that crisscrossed the market floor. There was a stink of vegetables, meat and raw seafood in the air.

In one corner of the market, near the flower and plant stalls, were the hawkers with their soups, noodles, rice dishes and various drinks. We went to Celery Chang's stall and bought a glass of iced lime juice each. It was so cold it hurt my throat: that's how I liked it.

Someone came up and offered to sell us a scarf.

'No, thanks,' I said.

'What about the boy?' asked the seller.

Blindboy asked, 'What colour are they, Hotwire?'

'Brown,' I said, 'you wouldn't like them.'

48

'Naw,' Blindboy agreed. 'I hate yerky brown. I like to wear reds and greens.'

The scarf seller went away looking puzzled that a blind person should care about colours, but Blindboy really did care what he was wearing.

'Even if I can't see it,' he had once told me, 'other people can. I don't want to be seen in yellow, brown or purple.'

While we were sipping our drinks, an old woman struggled past us with one of those big Chinese flowerpots. In it was a giant fern that was swishing in everyone's faces as she staggered around, trying to carry the great plant towards the entrance to the market.

'Can you help me, little boy?' she asked me.

'I'm a girl,' I said, running my fingers through my short hair, 'and I'm not little. I'm thirteen.'

But I remembered what John Woo had told us about being polite to people, especially elderly people, and that we should show them our best manners.

'Where do you want to take it to?' I asked.

'Just to the entrance of the market,' puffed the old woman. 'Can your friend help, too?'

'Oh, I guess it will be all right,' I replied. 'Blind-boy, can you get the other side of this pot?'

Blindboy did as he was asked and when I said, 'One, two, three . . .' we both lifted it off the ground.

49

'Just walk forward,' I said to Blindboy. 'We're following an old woman.'

She led us to the market exit.

Once there she stepped out into the street and looked along it. I guessed she was searching for her bender. Sure enough a large bender drew away from a parking space down the road and drove towards us. It was a pretty swazz job with tinted windows. The old woman was obviously well off.

When the bender drew up alongside us, she went around the back and opened the hatchback door.

'Can you heave it round here, kids?' she asked. 'Pop it into the back of the bender?'

'Forward,' I groaned, my muscles screaming. 'It's just a few yards away, Blindboy.'

'I'll make it worth your while,' said the woman.

Now that we were in the light of day, she looked familiar to me. I'd seen this woman somewhere before and thought perhaps she was a regular customer at the market.

She was a terrible dresser. The hem of her skirt was hitched up at the back about three inches higher than the front. Her tights were all wrinkled around the ankles. The bottom of her blouse was poking through her coat. She was a mess. When she walked in her high-heeled shoes, she looked like she would fall flat on her face if she leaned forward.

Blindboy and me humped the great pot up into the hatchback, while the woman held the door open, then pushed the fronds inside.

'Come round to the side of the bender,' she murmured, 'and you can have your reward.'

She was fiddling inside her handbag at the time and I thought, we're going to get a good tip here!

It was when we were huddled around the driver's door that it happened.

'Here you are, Hotwire,' she said.

I looked up into her face.

'Hey, how do you know my name?'

The passenger door suddenly flew open. A huge man jumped out and grabbed me, throwing me into the bender. I gave out a yell, which startled Blindboy into running. The old woman kicked off her shoes and raced after him, grabbing him within a few paces. She was obviously stronger than she looked as she hauled Blindboy, struggling and kicking, back to the bender. She and the big man threw Blindboy onto the seat next to me.

I tried opening the other passenger door.

It was locked.

The big man got into the bender at the back, while the old woman jumped into the front passenger's seat.

At that moment Mr Singh, Mrs Chau Hai and Miss Patel came running out of the market, having

51

realized we were being kidnapped, and tried to pull open the doors to the bender.

They were, of course, all now locked.

The driver chuckled and sped away, leaving John Woo's friends looking after us through the unsettled dust.

The driver of the bender looked into the rear view mirror at us and I recognized him immediately.

'Mouseman!' I cried.

'That's *sir* to you,' sneered Mouseman. 'I want you and Blindboy to meet my new associate, Grote.'

I stared at the big man sitting next to me. He smiled and revealed the gaps between his teeth. What fascinated me most about his features was his nose. One minute it was there, then it wasn't. He had the ability to turn it inside out, like one of those on a hollow mask. When he sniffed, his nose went into his face with a *pop*. When he blew down his nostrils, it popped out again. He laughed as he did this trick.

'Is he a kerk?' asked Blindboy. 'This Grote?'

'Worse than a kerk,' I replied. 'He's not even human – he's got a face made of rubber.'

'You watch it,' growled Grote. He wrenched the metal handle off the inside of the door and with an amazing show of brute force, he twisted it into what looked like an earring for a lady who liked to wear chunky jewellery.

'That's one door we won't be able to get out of,' I said. 'He's gone and busted it.'

'I'll bust your head,' growled the bear beside me.

Mouseman laughed. 'Take no notice of them, Grote. They'll try to wind you up all the time, if you let them. They'll be hoping to make you mad so that you won't be concentrating – then they'll try to escape.'

The old woman turned round at that moment, her make-up smudged over her face. She pulled off a grey wig revealing brown straggly hair. Then she put on some glasses. Finally she pulled some cotton wool from out of her mouth and I saw that her teeth looked quite goofy without the padding in her cheeks.

'Hello, kids,' she said, a little sadly.

I recognized her – no, *him* – then, much too late of course. He was a computer expert, one of Mouseman's old gang.

'Tweedle,' I said. 'I thought you'd gone straight after they threw Mouseman in jail.'

'He did,' growled Mouseman, 'but now I've caught him and bent him again. I need him for a job – just as I need you two.'

'So this isn't revenge?' Blindboy said, relief in his voice. 'You're not going to kill us?'

'Not yet,' sneered Mouseman, sitting small and compact behind the wheel of the bender. 'Maybe

I'll kill you afterwards. I need you to do something for me first.'

'We won't do it,' I replied, determinedly.

'Oh, yes you will,' he said softly. 'Oh, yes you will.'

5

'I feel sick,' I said.

The bender sped along, over the high, curving bridge across the river. On either side of the bridge, along the banks of the wide city river, was a wasteland of concrete and metal. The wharves and quays were no longer used and were derelict.

'None of your tricks, missy,' said Mouseman.

Nothing makes me more mad than being called *missy*.

I bit my tongue hard. The pain shot through my head. It would make me go pale. Then I deliberately held my breath for a minute and a half. When I was satisfied I spoke again.

'I really do feel like throwing up,' I moaned. 'I think I'm going to puke right here in the bender . . .'

Mouseman shot a look at me and obviously didn't like what he saw. 'You hold that back,' he yelled. 'I can't stand kids being sick.'

I began to dry retch.

Blindboy said, 'She always gets like this – it's motion sickness. Last time she'd been eating brussels and yellow-stained fish balls. It was *horrible . . .'*

Mouseman looked in the rear view mirror at Blindboy and narrowed his eyes. 'How did *you* know they were *yellow-stained* fish balls?'

'I smelled 'em.'

Mouseman swerved the bender across three lanes of fast-moving traffic. Skidders, benders and wazzoos blared their horns at him and flashed their lights. Mouseman shook his fist at them all. He stopped the bender on the high point of the massive bridge, got out and dragged me to the parapet, making me lean over.

'Be sick now,' he said.

I knew I couldn't *actually* do it, but my barfing noises must have been quite convincing, because Mouseman looked away with a disgusted expression on his face.

I stared down into the murky water, far below. It was a sort of browny-yellow colour with flecked foam: the factories all dumped their waste in this river. There was some raw sewage that went into its waters too. People tell you that if you fall in the river you need about thirty injections against all sorts of diseases, from typhoid to dysentery. A dead dog floated by while I stared down into the creeping waters. Even the seagulls wouldn't eat from the river.

I knew Blindboy couldn't run. He would be hit by a wazzoo or bender. It was up to me to escape, so that I could get the police to search for Mouseman's hideout. I hated leaving Blindboy with Mouseman, but I didn't have any choice. It didn't make sense for both of us to be captives.

'Come on, hurry up,' growled Mouseman beside me. 'Get it all out and then let's get going.'

I took a deep breath, made sure there were no barges or boats underneath, and then said, 'Bye bye, ratface.'

I fell all the way forwards until I was tumbling through the space between the bridge and the water. On the way down I could hear Mouseman yelling something. I don't think he was praying for my safe landing. I did three lazy somersaults, watching the factory chimneys swim around the sky. When I hit the water it smacked all the air out of me; it felt as if I'd struck concrete.

Going under, down into the warm water was like sinking in sludge. I tried to keep my mouth closed, but I wasn't very sure which was up and which was down, and so took a breath too quickly. I swallowed liquid that would burn through a barge bottom and soil a cargo of slaughterhouse bones. Now I really *did* feel sick. The bile rose to my throat and I added to the river's pollution, gagging as the current swept me along.

But I was *alive*. And maybe all those years on the dump, eating swill, would be enough to make me immune. The river bacteria would have to be supergerms to get *me*.

Although I'd never been a good swimmer I could keep on top of the water. I let the current take me, twisting and swirling, wherever it was going. It finally washed me up on a deserted dock side. I crawled out of the shallows and lay on my back in the sunlight, gasping for breath. Around me, like tall man-eating insects, were the rusting remains of derricks and cranes. They seemed to be bending over me purposely, thinking about whether I would make a decent meal or not.

I must have passed out then, because when I woke it was night-time.

It wasn't so dark that I couldn't see the shapes of broken down warehouses, all around me. The derricks were still visible too, still leaning over me, cold and curious. I could hear the rattling of loose corrugated metal sheets in the wind, the clanging of a bell, the creaking of giant crane hooks swinging in the night winds.

Here and there were the whispers of rats, scurrying over rotting tarpaulin.

It seemed an eerie, dead place; windswept and empty. There were no boats or ships moored at the quays or wharves. Oil drums stood in stacks, seemingly undisturbed for a century. There was the odd pile of buoys here and there. Coils of rusting chains, some attached to anchors, lay in heaps. Containers sat empty, flaking red dust.

'Some dump,' I said to myself, to keep my spirits up. 'Nothing even worth taking.'

I stood up and turned to face the moon, which was big and round on the horizon. Hard dark edges cut across the grey concrete, dividing the ground into sectors. It gave the landscape a crazy appearance, sharp with moonshadows. For a moment I thought I saw a shape moving along one of the stacks of buoys. My blood froze.

'Dogs,' I muttered. 'Packs of dogs.'

I turned again to hurry away – and almost stepped over the edge of the dock into the river. I stared at the black waters. There were no boats out there. It was probably a backwater canal, an off-shoot of the main river, no longer used.

I felt as if I were on another planet, with no people around. It was weird.

Making my way through the rusting heaps of chains, I went in a direction I thought would lead me out of the docklands. What I actually did was stumble around a corner into some light. There were about a dozen fires there, with hunched figures around them. Since it was warm weather the fires must have been for cooking and seeing by, not for warmth. I turned to go but a dark shape came at me and grabbed me.

'Wass this then, eh? What we got 'ere?'

I looked up into the smooth but dirty features of a slim young man. He was obviously a vagrant. Underneath all the grime he was probably quite handsome, but to me he looked like a snake about to strike. His grip was strong – wiry and strong – and his eyes glittered redly, like those of a rat caught in the light of a torch. Shadows emphasized his sunken cheeks.

'Hey, let me go, you kerk!' I yelled.

Now some other figures came running from the fires; children and adults. They studied me with strange, hungry expressions. Like the man who held me, they all wore filthy rags and smelled as if they hadn't bathed for a year. I used to smell like that when I lived on the dump, but my nose had become more sensitive since living in the Golden Arcade.

The children and some of the women started pinching my arms and legs.

'Not a lot of meat on 'im,' said one woman.

'*Her*,' I corrected. 'I'm a girl. Get off. Get your dirty paws off me.'

Instead they dragged me over to an old river buoy, lying at an angle on the cracked concrete. The top half of the buoy was a cage where a warning bell used to swing. There was a little gridded gate in the front. They pushed me through the opening into the very tight-fitting cage. Then they locked the gate with a rusty old padlock.

I almost filled the whole of the cage with my body. It was such a tight fit in there, some of me was poking through the iron cage. The children kept poking these parts with their sticks. I could see the rags were so rotten on their backs, they were dripping bits of cloth where they walked.

This was one of those forgotten places, where the people were at starvation level.

I decided they were going to *eat* me.

A skinny woman with folded arms came up to the cage. 'Where you from, boy?' she asked, fiddling with her greasy shawl. 'Where are your folks?'

I decided it was hopeless worrying about whether they thought I was a boy or girl.

'I live in the Golden Arcade,' I said. 'John Woo is my grandfather.'

One of the men looked up sharply at this remark. 'You're a liar,' he said. 'John Woo is Chinese. You ain't Chinese.'

'I'm adopted,' I said, relieved that someone had heard of John. 'He's my adopted grandpa.'

Someone hit the cage with a stick. 'Quiet!' they yelled. 'Who asked you to speak?'

They left me alone after that and tended their fires. Since it was a hot night, I was sweltering. The heat from the nearest fire was making the cage bars too hot to touch, but I couldn't help touching them. No-one seemed much interested in me now. At least they weren't looking at me and licking their lips any more. They seemed to be waiting for something, staring at the river every so often, listening and watching.

Later, as I was trying to sleep, I heard the sound of a motor launch coming up the river. Sure enough, a sleek-looking black yacht drifted into a quay and moored there. Shortly after that two men walked into the light of the fires.

'OK, Dave,' said one of the men, 'what have you got for us tonight?'

A sack was thrust in front of the man and he began rummaging through it, taking out all sorts of shiny objects. Some bargaining went on between Dave, the man who had grabbed me in the first place, and the two newcomers. The medium of exchange – that's what it's called I think – was food. So many barrels of pork chops for a silver chalice, so many chickens for a fancy clock, so many loaves of bread for a picture.

'Anything else?' asked one of the newcomers, after going through the sack's contents.

'Yeah,' said Dave, 'we got a boy here. We'll sell 'im to you, cheap.'

'I thought you used all your robber kids,' said the man.

'This one doesn't thieve,' said Dave. 'We fished 'im out of the river today, so he's quite fresh. You could sell him on, over where you're goin'.'

The man stroked his bearded chin. 'I don't know – kidnapping? That's a very serious offence. And the slave trade isn't what it used to be, you know. Now if the kid had been a girl . . . they're looking for girls to do intricate work – their fingers are smaller than boys', and quicker.'

'I think she is a girl,' said the old woman with the shawl, quickly. 'I think she is.'

62

'Make up your mind,' growled the second man. 'Is it a girl or a boy?'

'I'm a girl,' I yelled, before I'd thought too much about it. Then, when I realized I was going to be taken away, down river to the sea and then over it, to be sold to some farmer out in the wilderness of the inner continents, I knew I should have been protesting that I was in fact a *boy*, and not so easy to sell. 'I can thieve though,' I yelled, shaking my prison bars. 'I'm good at stealing, Dave. You just try me! I'm great at hotwiring skidders and benders. That's what they call me – Hotwire. You should see some of the . . .'

'Naw,' Dave replied. 'John Woo's an honest man. His gran'child wouldn't thieve.'

'Yes, I would. I haven't been adopted very long. That's where he got me from – the sweatshops. He had to adopt me so's he could make me work in his computer shop. I'd rather be thieving, like I always used to. It's much easier.'

The man with the beard said, 'So the girl's an orphan? Well, that makes it easier to pass her on. No parents to come looking for her. Police won't be upset about an orphan. Plenty of those in the streets. I know someone looking for a girl with small, quick hands.'

'Big,' I said, spreading my palms and fingers. 'Great big hands – and very slow. Arthritis. Got it as a baby.'

'Inventive too,' smiled the man. 'OK, we'll

63

take her – six cabbages and a chicken. All right?'

'I'm worth more than six cabbages,' I yelled. 'Don't you take that for me, Dave. I'll steal you a dozen skidders tomorrow. I'll make you a rich man.'

Dave sighed and said to the bearded man, 'I'll take the cabbages and chicken, Jake. Get rid of her, quick. She's a pain in the ear.'

I looked at Dave. 'I was scared. I thought you were going to eat me,' I said.

He winced. 'I wouldn't eat you if you was wrapped in silver paper and looked like roasted turkey. What d'you think we are, cannibores?'

I think he was mixing cannibals up with carni-vores.

'Yes, I thought so.'

He looked me up and down again and grim-aced. 'Yuk!' he said.

They came and unlocked the cage and took me to the sleek black yacht. I was dragged on board and locked in a small toilet that smelled only a bit less stinky than the river. There, I sat on the edge of the toilet and brooded, wondering if I would get a chance to make a break for it, before they put me on a larger vessel and sent me to some hell-factory abroad.

I heard them yelling to cast off and then the engines gave a velvety growl and we were on the move.

We went ploughing through the water, more or

less in a straight line as far as I could judge from the movements. After about half-an-hour I began to feel a bit ill. The boat was swaying from side to side, and going up and down. It was climbing hills, falling into valleys, rocking back and forth as it did so. Finally, I was sick in the toilet.

Then all of a sudden, the motors stopped, but we still seemed to be cutting through the water. I guessed we were now sailing through across the ocean.

'Let me out!' I yelled, but no-one came.

An hour later the boat began rocking violently again. I heard people running up and down gangways. Once again, I yelled to be let out, and finally some footsteps stopped outside the door to the toilet. The door flew open.

It was the bearded man, whom Dave had called Jake.

'You used to work on computers, kid?'

'Yes, Jake,' I replied, seeing no sense in lying.

'Come with me,' he ordered, 'I've got a job for you – you do this right and we'll let you go free.'

I followed him, still groggy on my feet, to the wheelhouse on top of the yacht.

6

There were two other men besides Jake in the wheelhouse, both looking tired, harassed and confused. One was wearing a captain's cap. The other was the kerk who had been with Jake when he went to trade with Dave and his dockland hobos.

In the distance I could see the twinkling of lights on a far shore. We were out at sea somewhere. I guessed the lights were at the place where we had come from, not where we were going to, since we hadn't been at sea that long.

'You know about computers, kid?' asked the man in a captain's cap. 'Can you fix our computer?'

'What does the computer *do*?' I asked.

'Never you mind, kid,' said Jake's sidekick, a kerk with hardly any forehead between his hair and his eyes. 'You do like the captain says. You just fix the computer, see?'

I looked at this moron and shook my head. 'I can't fix it until I know what it does. What am I supposed to make it do? Fry burgers?'

He took a step forward. 'You watch it . . .' but Jake moved in to stop him.

'The kid's right, Largo. She needs to know.' He turned to me. 'It controls the whole vessel. If we don't get it fixed, we'll drift until we land up on some rocks somewhere. See that sail?' He pointed through the windscreen. I could see a tall oblong sail fashioned from fibreglass, attached to a movable mast. 'We set the course from in here and the computer continually adjusts the sail so that it takes the best advantage of any wind which will take us along that course.'

'You mean, you decide the general direction to take and the computer makes the fine adjustments, according to the position of the wind?' I said, sounding swazz even to myself.

The captain looked at the other two men. 'This kid knows what she's talking about. She's no drummo.'

I was also good at playing computer pirate games.

'What about the engine?' I asked. 'Why don't you use the engine?'

Largo looked disgustedly at Jake, who in turn looked down at his feet.

'Because this kerk forgot to load the fuel – we're out of gas.'

'And the ship-to-shore communications?'

'They need the computer up and running.'

'Oh,' I said. Then, 'You got any tools? I'll need some maintenance instruments.'

They produced a wallet bristling with computer tools.

'You'll set me free, afterwards – right?'

'Sure, kid, sure. You fix the computer and – er – we'll let you go the minute we hit land,' said Jake, trying to look as saintly as possible.

Yeah, I thought, and all the orphans on the city dump will get a box of chocolates from the mayor at Christmas time.

Fat chance.

Still, if I was to get out of this mess, the yacht had to be repaired, otherwise we'd all die.

I got to work on their computer, taking off the front panel and pulling out the boards, until I had the whole guts of the thing exposed. I could see at once what the trouble was: salt sea spray had corroded one of the terminals. But I wanted to take as long as possible over this, so they would all be exhausted by the time I repaired it.

'This is going to take some time,' I said. 'On the software side, the hard disk is cluttered with bad clusters and will have to be unclogged and the files saved under a set of series zero. On the hardware side, several motivator chips have been crosswired to the rocker board. These wouldn't be so bad if someone hadn't filled the spare hard disk space to capacity – it'll have to be drained and reactivated.'

I looked up with a frown and said in a chiding tone, 'When was this computer last serviced?'

The men all looked at each other and shrugged.

'Well, who makes the checks?' I asked.

The captain blinked and said, 'I can work it all right – when it's up and running – but I don't know anything about servicing or checking it. I just know how to set a course on the program . . .'

I sighed and pretended to get to work. 'That's the trouble with people these days – they think because they can drive a skidder they know all about vehicles on the road. Same thing with computers. The public needs to educate itself on what goes on *inside* an engine – or a computer.'

Largo realized he was being told off.

'That's enough lip, kid,' he said, sternly. 'Just get on with the repairs. I don't like being told I'm a drummo.'

I did as I was told.

I dragged out the repairs, and added a few secret adjustments of my own, until the men around me looked as tired as I felt.

'That's it,' I said. 'You shouldn't have any more trouble with it – but I'd better stay up here in the wheelhouse, just in case the computer should go down before dawn.'

The captain switched on the system and found it was working perfectly. 'Throw the kid in the brig,' he said.

But Largo overruled him. 'You heard what the kid said, it might go down again. Let her sleep on the deck up here. Where can she go? We're way out at sea.'

Largo then turned to me.

69

'What's your name, kid – Hotwire, isn't it? Well, Hotwire, you sleep in the corner of the wheelhouse. No tricks, you hear? Once we get to land, I'll let you go.'

Yeah, and the mayor's chocolates will have a thousand dollar bill inside each one, I thought.

Fat chance.

'Can I use one of those life jackets as a pillow?' I asked. 'The deck's pretty hard.'

'Sure, kid – but remember, no tricks.'

Largo tossed me a lifesaver.

I fell asleep in the corner of the wheelhouse and slipped into a nice comfortable dream about food. I was woken by angry shouts about two hours later. It was grey dawn. All three men were standing nearby, wrestling with the wheel to the rudder.

'I can't shift it!' cried the captain. 'The sail must have jammed. I've been trying to turn the wheel now for about half an hour – then I woke you two.'

'You shouldn't have fallen asleep in the first place,' yelled Largo at him. 'You should have stayed awake.'

'Oh yeah, why not *you*?'

'It was your watch!' shouted Jake.

'I just dozed for a few minutes, for smiff's sake.'

'And the rest,' said Jake.

'Stop arguing and do something. We're heading towards the damn harbour wall,' growled Largo.

With both eyes open now I studied the legs, milling around me. When I was sure of a free path to the open door of the bridge I jumped to my feet. Then I ran out on to the deck. There were shouts behind me. I slipped on the life jacket. Jumping up onto the gunwales I studied the choppy water below me. It looked green, cold and *very* deep.

'Get her!' screamed Jake.

The yacht, with a stiff wind behind it, was swiftly approaching the harbour to the city. I would not have far to swim. I threw myself into the churning green water.

Smiff! Even though it was summer this was ocean water and pretty cold. The shock of it made my eyes hurt for a moment. My head went under and I tasted salt. Then I bobbed to the surface and stayed there, the waves lifting me and dropping me gently, while the yacht sped on towards the harbour wall.

I smiled grimly. 'Got you, you kerks.'

When I had repaired the computer, I had time-set it to alter the boat's course. I had prepared it so that after about an hour the sails would automatically change the direction of the boat. While I was fast asleep, and the crew were all dozing, the yacht had done a wide, gentle U-turn until it was sailing back towards the twinkling harbour lights.

Once it was on a straight course for home the computer had locked the rudder.

To change direction the crew would have had

to reprogram the computer and I knew none of them could do that.

As the current now carried me along the shore, I saw the beautiful black yacht smash into the harbour wall. The bows just splintered and crumpled. I saw three figures jump overboard. Then the boat sank down into the murky depths of the sea. I had destroyed about a million dollars' worth of yacht: those three kerks were not going to be happy with me.

I forgot about them as I was carried up-river. The tide was on the flow now, so I was caught in a fast current going inland. One or two people on the bank saw me being swept along, but the flow was so fast I was there and gone, before they could do anything about it. Perhaps they would report it to someone, if they could spare the time, but you couldn't trust them to do it.

This was the second time I'd fallen in the polluted yellow river, thick with factory waste and raw sewage.

I went shooting past the dockyard where Dave and his tribe of thieves lived and eventually reached a residential district where the lawns of big houses went right down to the water's edge. The current slowed down at this point and carried me in towards the bank. There was an old man bent over some flower beds with a trowel in his hand. I yelled to him.

'Hey, mister – get me out – I'm drowning!'

He looked up as he saw me drifting towards him. His eyes opened wide and then he ran to the water's edge where there was a rowing boat. Out of the dinghy he took a long pole with a hook on the end. With this he fished around my neck, catching me on the collar, and dragged me to the edge.

Coughing and spluttering I crawled out of the river and flopped onto the bank.

'Lucky I had the boat hook handy,' he said, 'or you might have been a goner.'

'Thanks, mister,' I wheezed, all my strength drained away. 'I appreciate this.'

'What on earth were you doing in the river, child?'

I looked up into his kindly old face and saw a genuine concern there: not something you often witness in the eyes of the people in this city. He had bushy white eyebrows, a white cropped beard and thin white hair. His face was as black as charcoal and shiny with goodwill. He smiled a reassuring smile at me as I stared up at him.

'You remind me of my grandfather,' I said. 'John Woo.'

'Do I?' he grinned. 'Well, probably the only thing we have in common is old age, I suspect.'

'No, he's a swazz man too,' I told him.

He looked pleased at this and nodded his head.

'Now,' he said, 'you still haven't answered my question. What were you doing in the river?'

I thought about telling him the truth and then decided against it. The story was pretty long and complicated and I wasn't sure it would have sounded real. So I shortened it.

'I was caught by some child slavers,' I said, 'and put on a boat. I managed to grab a life jacket and jump overboard.'

'Child slavers?' He looked at me dubiously, but then shrugged and said, 'Well, good for you. You got away. Now what do I do with you? I've got to be somewhere important in a few minutes. Can I trust you in the house?'

'What do you mean?' I asked.

He looked at me hard and then said, 'Nothing – forgive an old man's suspicious mind. You come up to the house, get dried and warm, and then wait for me to come back. All right? My name's Jeremy, but people call me Jem. What about you?'

'I'm Hotwire.'

He looked impressed. 'That's a really fancy name – dramatic! I like it. I wish I had a name like that, but my mother named me after my father, who was named Jeremy after his father before him . . .'

'I like Jem,' I said. 'It sounds expensive.'

He laughed. 'Oh, like *gem*, you mean?'

Which confused me, but I let it go.

I nodded, gratefully. We went up to this swazz house together. It had more windows than a museum and twice as many rooms. Where did someone get this much money, to own a house this size? I said to the old man, 'This is a big place.'

He nodded. 'I don't own it,' he said, answering one of my questions without me having to ask it. 'I used to, but I had to sell it about twenty years ago. I'm the manager now. It belongs to the National Heritage people. It's an old stately home. You won't find a place this big in private hands, these days, unless it's way outside the city limits.'

'Is it open to the public?' I asked.

'No, no. It's a kind of a hotel. It's used by government officials as a conference and business centre. They come here for their meetings with important visitors from overseas and such.'

'You look after it all by yourself?'

He smiled again. 'When it's needed for an official function, I hire in staff from an agency. At the moment we're in a quiet period. It's not due to be used again for at least another month. I think they're getting rid of me before then, in any case.'

'Getting rid of you?' I cried. 'What for?'

'Too old, I guess. Being the former owner, I was supposed to be manager in perpetuity – that means until I pop my cork – die – but someone seems to have lost the contract. I kept it in a vault at the bank, but it's disappeared.'

'That's yerky,' I said. 'Sounds like dirty dealing to me. Sounds like the creasers are moving in.'

He shrugged. 'Well, there doesn't seem to be much I can do about it, so I'll have to go into some small hotel somewhere – or an old folks' home. We'll see. Nothing for you to worry about, young lady. You get dried now. Put your clothes on those big radiators in the bathroom. I'll leave them turned on for you.'

'All right. Thanks, Jeremy.'

'That's Jem, to you.'

'John Woo, my adopted grandfather, told me to always be extra polite and respectful to old people.'

Jem nodded. 'That sounds good, but I really *want* to be called *Jem*.'

'You got it, Jem,' I said.

'Now I've got to go,' he told me.

He left the house a few moments later and I went up the grand staircase to this swazz bathroom the size of a warehouse. The taps and fittings looked as if they were made of gold, but were probably only gilt. They were really tricky to work, being sort of big and old-fashioned in shape, but I eventually got the hang of it. I wrapped a big towel around myself while my clothes were drying on the radiators. Then, after a bath I dressed again and went on the prowl for food.

I guessed an old man wouldn't have Frizzo and bamburgers in the house, but I hoped for some biscuits and cheese.

While I was rooting around in the fridge the front door bell rang.

7

I opened the door.

'Say,' said the man standing there, 'we've just moved in next door, and I wonder . . .'

The man's eyes opened wide on seeing me standing before him.

I was likewise startled and my surprise turned to horror.

'Grote?' I yelled, and tried to slam the door.

Grote was quick for a big man – very quick. His foot came out and kicked the door wide open. His hand flashed out and grabbed me around the throat. His head jutted forward and he glared at me from about two centimetres away.

'Got you, you slummer!' he said, triumphantly. He stared around me at the empty hallway to the house. 'You alone?'

I yelled. 'No – help, Jem – help me . . .'

Grote stood there as if made from solid rock. When no-one came out of the bowels of the house he grinned.

'Oh dear, no-one else home? Good. You're coming with me, to meet the boss. He'll be pleased to see you, girl.'

'My name's Hotwire,' I grunted, struggling with the hand that clutched my throat. It was like a steel vice. There was no way I was going to escape that grip. 'You call me by my name, Grote.'

'Yeah, all right, girlie.'

Grote dragged me down the steps and across the lawn to a hole in the hedge. This was presumably the gap he had used to enter Jem's garden. He pulled me through the hedge and marched me up to the French doors to the next house. In the room beyond, I could see Mouseman standing, watching me being hauled into his house. He actually rubbed his hands together in glee.

'You got Hotwire?' he cried, as I was thrust into the room. 'Where did you get her?'

'She was in the house next door,' snarled Grote. 'I went to see if they had a phone working. Ours is out of order. She said somethin' about a guy named Jem.'

'That's Jeremy to you,' I said, rubbing my sore neck. 'When he gets home all hell will be let loose.'

Mouseman stared at me for a while then said, 'I don't think so. This is someone she's managed to con for an hour or two. Once they find her gone they'll heave a sigh of relief and thank their stars that she's no longer on their property. I know this girl – she's an expert at picking up temporary guardians.'

'Ha, well, that's where you're wrong – this man's a long-lost uncle, see.'

'Yeah, yeah,' yawned Mouseman, wearily. 'I've heard it all before. Grote, take her down to the cellar where we're keeping Blindboy. Show her what we expect of girls called "Hotwire".'

I wondered what Mouseman meant, as Grote opened a door under the stairs and marched me down some stone steps.

The cellar had a soft yellow glow about it. There were wine racks stacked against one wall, complete with full bottles, hundreds of them. In three corners of the stone-clad room were barrels and other junk.

In the fourth corner there was a heap of dollars, like a pile of autumn leaves, mixed up with a few papers. I guessed the mound of money was the loot from the bank robbery. Mouseman was an untidy kerk, even when it came to millions of dollars. He left it about like someone else would leave small change. I think he believed he was being cool.

However, what interested me the most was a long, heavy table in the middle of the cellar.

Standing on one side of this table was Blindboy, looking thin and peaky.

On the other side was Tweedle, wearing a dust coat and looking every centimetre the technician.

Between them were some familiar objects: bits

of cybercats, like those we had let loose in the alleys.

'Blindboy,' I said. 'You all right?'

Blindboy cocked his head towards me, listening to my footsteps. He sniffed the air, knowing not only the sound of my tread, but my smell. 'Hot-wire? They got you?'

'Yeah, 'fraid so. Pretty yerky, eh? Are these kerks treating you OK?'

'They won't let us have any food, unless we help them.'

'That's right,' said Grote. 'You do as you're told and you get fed – if you don't, you starve.'

I was already pretty hungry. I hadn't eaten in twenty-four hours and it felt like my heart was sticking to my ribs. If I didn't get something in my stomach soon, I would begin eating myself, start-ing with my fingers. Blindboy looked as if he were in the same position as me. He kept licking his lips too.

'You thirsty, Blindboy?' I asked.

'Yeah, a bit. They won't let me drink, either. What about you?'

'I've got half the river inside me,' I grumbled. 'I've swallowed enough industrial waste to kill a whale.'

Grote swore and said, 'Except that you're not a whale – poisons don't affect giant sewer rats like you.'

'You watch your language, Grote,' said the

weedy, goofy Tweedle, unexpectedly coming to my rescue. 'Listen, kids, it's best if you do as Mouseman says. We have to make some more of those electro-mechanical cats you've put on the streets . . .'

'The cybercats?' I said.

'Yes, if that's what you call them. Mouseman wants to use them as robots with which to rob houses. He intends sending them in through cat doors. They're to be programmed to look for diamonds and gold – jewellery.'

'How do we do that?' I said. 'What does he want from us – magic?'

Mouseman growled. 'If that's what it takes, yes.'

He had come down the cellar steps behind me, as silently as one of the creatures after which he was named. He was carrying a tray full of bamburgers and cans of Frizzo. My stomach rumbled and I grabbed at a burger. 'Here, Blindboy,' I said, 'catch . . .' I tossed him one.

Blindboy snatched at the air in front of him, judging it just right, catching the burger before it hit the table in front of him.

'How does he do that?' Grote said, shaking his head in amazement. 'Are you sure the kid's blind?'

'Absolutely,' snapped Blindboy. 'I do it by sound, you kerk – just because I've got no eyes doesn't mean I can't do the things you can do.

81

Objects make a noise when they go through the air. I hear and I pounce, see.'

Blindboy snatched at a fly buzzing past with his free hand and caught it. Then he let it go. Grote tried to catch it in the same way, but missed. It flew up and out of the cellar.

'Hey,' Grote said. 'That's pretty good – the kid's pretty good, Mouseman. I couldn't hear the burger go through the air.'

'That's because you're not *him*,' said Tweedle. 'Blindboy has super-sensitive hearing.'

'All right, that's enough talking,' Mouseman grunted. 'Hotwire, Blindboy and Tweedle – you get to work. I want those cats yesterday, understand? Make them look exactly like the ones you put out on the streets. That way no-one will be able to tell the difference between a robber cybercat and one that eats rubbish.'

Tweedle said to Blindboy, 'How do we start?'

Blindboy asked him, 'You read Braille?'

'No.'

'Then you better start learning if you want me to teach you anything. Hotwire reads Braille. You need it if you want to work with me.'

'Yeah,' I said, 'get learning, kerk.'

So, we didn't have any choice. We had to help Mouseman with his cats. We tried to delay things, Blindboy and me, by making up all sorts of problems. The trouble with Tweedle was, he knew what he was doing. Tweedle wasn't as brilliant as Blindboy and me with computers, but he knew enough to recognize when we were not working properly.

Later that day there was a ring on the front door bell. Mouseman came down into the cellar a little while later. He looked very smug. He told us that Jeremy had been to call, to ask after me.

'The old slummer wanted to know if we'd seen you,' Mouseman said, smirking. 'I told him I saw some hare-brained girl running off down the street. I advised him to go back to his house and check his property. I said you looked like one of those robber kids to me.'

'You ought to know,' snapped Blindboy. 'Being a yerky thief yourself.'

Mouseman glowered. 'You watch it, kid.'

He left us to our technical task. I have to say it, even though I was working on the wrong side of the law, I was still a brilliant technician. Within three days we had a prototype up and running. It was a cat just like our cybercats, only its eyes were cameras.

The new cybercat could be put into a house through a small opening. It could be remotely controlled and made to wander around the rooms. Its eyes would scan the contents of the rooms, and what it saw would appear on a screen in a parked bender outside in the street. When the operators in the bender saw something valuable, like a necklace, the cat could be made to go to the object and pick it up in its mouth.

'Well done, Tweedle,' Mouseman grunted. 'You did good.'

'*We* did the hard work,' I told him. 'It's us you should be thanking.'

'I wouldn't thank you two for pulling me out of the river if I was drowning,' replied Mouseman, frankly. 'I wouldn't thank you for a glass of water if I was dying of thirst.'

Blindboy and me were taken outside and into a bender. We were handcuffed to the door handles. Mouseman got in the back with our new cybercat. Grote drove the vehicle, while Tweedle operated the equipment from the front passenger's seat.

They found a suitable house and put the cat in through the cat flap on the side door.

Tweedle steered the cat into various rooms, using the remote control device. When he got the cat into the en suite bathroom, there was a gold watch lying on the shelf amongst the toothbrushes and nail scrubber. He got the cat to leap on the shelf, grab the watch in its jaws, and then come out of the house. A woman was coming up the stairs as the cybercat was going down.

'George?' she yelled to someone we couldn't see. 'There's a strange cat in the house.'

A voice came back over the cat-mike. 'Well, shoo it out then.'

Since the watch was inside the cat's mouth, the

woman couldn't see it, and she did as she was instructed. The cybercat allowed itself to be shooed out of the front door, where it met the resident feline. This creature was a big white Persian cat and it bristled instantly on confronting our cybercat. Our cat lifted its head slightly and squirted juice out of its nostrils into the Persian's face.

The juice had a bad egg smell.

The Persian was enraged and tried to swipe our cat with a clawed paw. The cybercat stood on its hind legs. Under the boggling eyes of the woman owner of the Persian, it expertly blocked the blow from the real cat with its left forepaw. Then it stepped forward and punched the Persian on the nose with its right forepaw, like a trained boxer at the Olympics.

'Yeah,' I said, for the benefit of Blindboy, 'a straight right to the jaw.'

Blindboy grinned. That move had been his idea.

You could see the surprise on the Persian's face on the screen and its eyes began to water.

The Persian screeched and ran through its owner's legs, into the house, presumably to find a place to hide. The house pet obviously did not approve of a cat which copied human fighting techniques. A rough and tumble with a spitting, clawing, biting beast was one thing: a stand-up fight with a device that should be opening cans in a kitchen was another.

'I thought you said it made all its moves like a cat?' snarled Mouseman. 'Tweedle?'

Tweedle said, 'They must have done that while I wasn't watching.'

'You're *paid* to watch them do *everything*,' Mouseman growled. 'If you're not careful I'll get Grote to stop your pocket money – you get my meaning? You sort that cat out. I don't want anyone suspecting it isn't a real cat.'

'Yes, sir,' whimpered the cowed Tweedle. 'Sorry, sir.'

On the whole though, Mouseman was pleased with our efforts. The cat deposited the gold watch into his hands and he put it on his own wrist straightaway. Then he got Grote to drive us home and told Tweedle to make a dozen more cybercats.

'Before the month is out, I want a thousand cats out there, robbing for me,' growled Mouseman.

When we got back to the house a question was asked. 'What about these two?' said Tweedle, pointing to Blindboy and me. 'What happens to them?'

'We don't need them any more,' Mouseman said, smiling greasily. 'Grote will tie their hands and feet together and dump them in the river with weights on them.'

'No!' exclaimed Tweedle, unexpectedly standing up to the master criminal. 'None of that, this time.'

'What do you mean?' snarled Mouseman, his

eyes narrowing. 'Are you trying to tell me my business, Tweedle?'

'I'm telling you, if you throw these kids in the river, you'll have to throw me in with them – then you'd have no-one to make your cybercats for you – or maintain them.'

'I might just consider it worth doing,' threatened Mouseman, but Tweedle stood resolutely in front of us.

I admired the technician for that. His own crimes stopped short of murder. Mouseman would have killed us and then eaten his supper without so much as a thought for anything but filling his stomach.

Tweedle was, at heart, not really cut out for crime.

8

Blindboy and me were kept chained in the cellar, while Tweedle and some other technicians he recruited worked on manufacturing more robber cybercats. Before the month was out there were a thousand cybercats looking just like our rubbish-eating cats, out there in the city stealing small valuables from people's apartments.

Mouseman quit the house one day, telling us he was leaving us in the cellar to starve. We watched as Tweedle and his gang of technicians packed their equipment into boxes and carried them up the stairs. Later that day Tweedle came to us.

'I've done all I can for you,' he said, wearing a hang-dog expression. 'It's up to you two now. I'm getting out. I'm flying abroad today. If I stay here, I'll have Mouseman on my back for the rest of my life – or have to live in a prison cell. I've had it, kids. Sorry. You're on your own.'

With that he left us and we didn't see anyone else for forty-eight hours.

Just when we were ready to gnaw our own wrists, Mouseman came to visit us, bringing some bread and water.

He laughingly showed us a newspaper.

The headlines read: VANISHED ORPHANS' CYBERCATS ROB MAYOR'S APARTMENT OF JEWELS.

The article went on to tell the gullible public that the orphans known as Hotwire and Blindboy had gone underground somewhere and from their hideout were operating their criminal cybercat network. *'The master crime boss John Woo has been imprisoned by the authorities,'* ran the article, *'but his two accomplices have yet to be tracked down and locked up with him.'*

'They've put John Woo in jail,' I said in an anguished tone to Blindboy. 'They think he's behind the robberies.'

Mouseman laughed hysterically. 'Yeah, ain't that a scream?' he said. 'Your Chinaman pal is doing time for *me* – I'm glad I let you live to see this after all. The look on your faces is worth a million in stolen credit notes.'

'You yerky kerk,' yelled Blindboy. 'If I ever get out of here, I'll make you sorry.'

'You need to grow up first,' snarled Mouseman, 'and then buy some eyes that work.'

'You just wait,' I said. 'We'll get you back.'

'Yeah, well, while you're thinking about that, chained to this floor, let me tell you something else. Your friend Tweedle seems to have disappeared. I'll find him eventually, but in the meantime I've recruited a new technician. He's fitting bombs inside all the robber cybercats. You remember my old plan to blast the city to pieces if the authorities didn't pay me a ransom?'

No wonder Tweedle had run away. He didn't want to be mixed up in any bombings. I couldn't blame him.

'I seem to remember,' I said, laughing into Mouseman's face, 'that Blindboy and me put a stop to that scheme.'

'That's right,' conceded Mouseman, 'but not this time. This time it'll work. One press of a button and a thousand cats will explode, taking buildings, streets and people with them. And guess who'll get the blame for it? The two little orphans and their adopted grandfather. Great scheme, eh?' He laughed. 'BOOOOOOOOOOM!'

'You're crazy,' I said, quietly.

'You're right, I am. Which means, of course, that I can dispose of you two when I feel like it. I might let you see a few cat bombs go up first, before getting rid of you.'

He turned, picked up an empty sack from the corner of the room and scooped the big pile of dollars into it. Then he began to sort through the heap of papers. After a while he grew impatient and kicked the rest aside.

'Deeds and mortgages,' he grumbled. 'I can't be bothered with these things – I'm going to rule the city soon.'

He heaved the bag of money onto his right shoulder and then turned to grin at us.

'Then again, I might not wait for any bombs to go off, before killing you two,' he said. 'That's the beauty of being in charge – I can change my mind at a moment's notice. It's going to be a great fourth of July, believe me.'

He left us, chuckling away to himself.

'We've got to get out of here, Blindboy,' I whispered. 'We've got to get these chains off.'

Blindboy said, 'I've been trying, but I can't do anything with the lock – how about you?'

'Naw, it's an old-fashioned key lock – not an electronic one. We need help.'

It would have been easy for me at that point, to go into the depths of despair, but Blindboy wouldn't let me. If there's one thing about him that's larger than life, it's his spirit. It's sort of bigger than his body, if you know what I mean. Blindboy has this scrawny little physique, but his spirit overflows it all round, and won't be stuffed inside its frame. Blindboy kept talking to me, asking me questions, telling me it was going to be all right, once we'd looked at all the possibilities.

'Is there a window nearby?' he asked me. 'I can feel a draught on my neck.'

I looked up. 'There's a stack of wine bottles behind us – wait a minute, I can see a faint glinting through them. Yes, maybe there is a window up there . . .'

When I peered through the rack of bottles, mostly dark red and rosy coloured wines, I could see a small circular window thick with dust making it almost opaque.

I told Blindboy about it.

'Casement window,' he said, surprising me. 'They're hinged in the middle.'

'How do you know that? You haven't lived in a house.'

'Video game,' he explained. '*The Casement Window*. It's one of those creepy house games.'

'Oh.'

We decided to try to get at the window, but had to pull the tall wine racks aside. Our chains were long enough to do this, but the racks were very heavy and unstable. When I yanked on the one in front of the casement window, it suddenly tore its bolts from the wall, teetered, and then fell forward.

'Look out!' I yelled at Blindboy.

I jerked on his chain and pulled him out of the way just as the rack of wines came crashing to the stone floor of the cellar. The noise was tremendous. Glass and liquid sprayed everywhere. Red wines flowed over the cellar floor, gurgling down a drain in the middle. When I helped Blindboy to his feet, the broken glass crunched under the soles of my old trainers.

We waited in apprehension, wondering if

someone would come down to the cellar to investigate, but they really must have all deserted the house, because no-one came. Mouseman hadn't even bothered to leave a guard there. Maybe he really did intend us to starve to death now?

Above my head now was the exposed casement window. It was filthy dirty and covered in cobwebs. I picked up the tall wine rack and leaned it against the wall. The last few bottles came tumbling from their holes and rolled across the stone floor. I used the empty rack like a ladder to climb up to the window. With my chain at full stretch I could just touch the bottom pane with my nose and peer out.

Licking the pane clean of grime with my tongue I could see down the length of the garden, which was at eye level.

There at the bottom was a tall dark figure with white hair and beard. He was staring at the house. I guessed he had heard the crash of the wine rack hitting the cellar floor.

'Jeremy!' I said.

'What?' asked Blindboy.

'That old man I told you about – the one who fished me out of the river – lives next door. He's at the bottom of the garden. He must have heard the wine rack go over. He's looking up here with a puzzled face . . .'

'Well, wave to him or something,' said the exasperated Blindboy. 'Yell at him.'

I yelled but I couldn't wave, since my hand wouldn't go over the windowsill.

Jeremy didn't seem to hear me. He turned to go through the hole in the hedge into his own garden.

'Quick, push over another rack of wines!' I shouted at Blindboy.

Blindboy did as he was asked, feeling along the walls and tugging a rack away from its rusted bolts. It came crashing down, narrowly missing him again. The noise was satisfyingly thunderous. Bottles shattered like crazy on the stone floor, wood splintered and broke, corks popped from fizzy champagne sounding like gunshots in the hollow cellar.

Staring through the window I could see that Jeremy had stopped in his tracks.

He turned slowly, then came walking up to the house.

'Yes! Yes! He's coming!' I cried.

I scrambled down the rack again and picked up a full bottle of wine. I hurled it as hard as I could at the casement window. It smashed through the glass, raining a few shards back on the pair of us. I didn't care, because a moment later Jeremy's face appeared in the hole above, framed by the shattered pane.

'What's going on here?' he asked, peering down at us. 'Who's that in there?'

'It's me, Jem – Hotwire. You remember? I've got a dram – dramatic name, you said.'

'Hotwire?' His face creased in recognition. 'What are you doing, throwing things through windows?'

I rattled my chains. 'We're prisoners down here – Mouseman, the criminal put us down here. We're chained to the walls and floor. Mouseman left us to starve.'

All this took a while to penetrate Jem's mind. I couldn't blame him. Even in this day and age people didn't chain kids like slaves in ancient times. Once he believed what he was being told, however, he moved fast enough. He went immediately and called the police.

'They're coming, Blindboy,' I said a while later, excitedly. 'I can hear them breaking down the doors.'

'Yeah,' said my adopted brother, 'they're coming, but remember what Mouseman said? The mayor thinks we're behind the robber cybercats. We'll just get arrested again. No-one will believe us about Mouseman, will they?'

I thought about this gloomy prospect and realized Blindboy was probably right.

However, the first face through the doorway of the cellar made me leap in joy.

'Jack?' I yelled.

And behind him came Phil Cannigan.

Jack Rickman and his partner, Phil, had obviously come back to the city, from the place to which they had been seconded.

Phil Cannigan shook his head, not at all impressed by Blindboy and me at the best of times.

'Would you look at those kids, Jack? We leave the city for five minutes and they manage to get themselves on a robbery charge and then chained to a cellar floor . . .'

'You all right, kids?' asked Jack, ignoring his partner.

'Thirsty,' said Blindboy, 'and hungry.'

A policeman came forward with a laser cutter, to free us from our chains.

Jack said, 'I'd like to know when you two are *not* hungry and thirsty – Phil, show 'em what we've brought them.'

Phil produced a package which when unwrapped proved to be Frizzos and bamburgers.

Once our chains were off we got stuck into the grub. I thanked Jeremy, who was standing just behind Phil, and introduced him to Jack. Jeremy said he had to go.

'I'm busy moving out of my house,' he said.

'Thanks for being a good citizen,' said Phil, stiffly.

'He's more than that,' I said. 'He's my friend, aren't you Jem?'

Jem smiled. 'Yes, I am. Now you look after yourself, Hotwire, you hear me? Stay away from that Mousemonster. And tell your grandfather he's a

lucky man to have grandchildren like you two –
you sure give a man some adventures.'

He chuckled and shook his head as he left.

'Grandfather?' said Jack. 'What grandfather?'

'John Woo is our official adopted grandfather,'
said Blindboy. 'So there.'

'Nothing to me,' said Jack, shifting his coat on
his shoulders in an embarrassed fashion. 'If he
wants to adopt a couple of street strays, that's up
to him.'

I knew why he was doing that, because we had
once asked him if *he* would adopt us, and he said
no. Jack said we would be more trouble than we
were worth, even though Barb would probably
have agreed. Barb, Jack's wife, was a doctor. They
were both busy people and they had a tiny apartment too small to allow them to adopt a kitten, let
alone two dump kids. I knew that, and didn't hold
it against him. Still, I knew he felt a bit guilty for
turning us down, though he went out of his way
to look in on us pretty often to make sure we were
all right.

Before we left the cellar I went over to the pile
of papers Mouseman had left. I knew they had
been stolen from the bank, when he and Grote had
robbed it of the two million dollars. I guessed the
robbers had just grabbed everything in the vault,
regardless of value. There was an idea in my head,
sparked off by something Mouseman had said
before leaving us that last time.

Deeds and mortgages.

'Come on,' Jack said. 'That's bank property there – you won't find any spare dollars for Frizzo. If I know Mouseman, he's taken every last note and coin.'

'I'm not looking for money,' I muttered.

Most of the papers were folded into thick wodges and tied with thin red ribbons. They had pompous looking titles on the front, in big black letters. Finally I came to the one I was looking for and held it up, triumphantly.

'Jem's contract,' I said. 'Mouseman stole it.'

'What?' Jack asked, looking puzzled.

'This is Jem's property,' I said, waving the contract under Jack's nose. 'I'm going to return it to him.'

Jack shrugged, as if to say, *who can fathom street kids?*

We were taken outside and I asked to go to Jem's house before we got into the police bender.

'Hurry up then,' muttered Phil. 'You kids are more of a nuisance than ten hardened criminals.'

I ran up the steps and rang the bell to Jem's residence.

He opened the door and peered down at me with his kindly face, smiling one of his warm smiles.

'You off then, Hotwire? Good luck to you.'

'I just wanted to thank you,' I said. 'For saving

me twice in a row – once from the river, and once from Mouseman.'

'It was a pleasure – believe me.'

'And I came to give you this,' I said, holding out the roll of papers I had in my hand. 'It's your contract. You don't need to move now. You can stay in your house as manager in perp – in perpil . . .'

'Perpetuity?' he said, looking amazed. 'But where did you get this?'

He took the papers and studied them for a moment, saying, 'Smiff! This is my contract, all right.'

'Mouseman stole it, along with a few million dollars. I guess he didn't think your house was worth much.'

'Only five million dollars,' laughed Jem. 'He's not as smart as he thinks he is. Thanks a bunch, Hotwire. You've paid me back in full. I saved your life, you saved mine.'

'I still owe you one,' I said.

He ruffled my hair. Normally I hate people doing that, but I put up with it from Jem.

'You owe me nothing,' he said. 'You've made an old man as happy as a lark.'

I walked back to the bender feeling as if I were queen of the city. Phil Cannigan stared at me impatiently, but I ignored him. Right at that moment I couldn't have cared less about a thick-eared cop with ants in his pants.

We roared away, into the stream of traffic.

'So what's this about you two manufacturing cybercats that rob houses?' asked Jack, sitting next to us.

Blindboy said, 'We did it under – under—'

'Under *duress*,' offered Phil Cannigan from the front seat.

'Yeah, that's it,' said Blindboy. 'We were *made* to do it by that kerk, Mouseman. He said he was going to tie us up and throw us in the river, if we didn't do as he told us.'

'And John Woo had nothing to do with it,' I told Jack. 'John Woo wasn't even with us.'

Jack looked thoughtful. 'So, let's get this story straight. First of all John Woo and you pair of hoodlums manufactured some rubbish-eating cybercats to clear the streets of trash, right?'

'Five thousand of them,' I said.

'Then Mouseman and Grote escaped from jail, captured you two, and put you to work making robber cybercats?'

'That's it,' said Blindboy, 'except that Hotwire escaped when we were first captured.'

'What happened?' he asked, turning to me.

'I jumped out of the bender, dived into the river, and was fished out by a crowd of dockland thieves. Some kerks with a black yacht bought me for six cabbages and a chicken. They said they were going to sell me overseas, to a slave trader. But their computer went wrong on the boat and they couldn't go anywhere. They asked me to fix it for them and I did, but I made it so the yacht did a wide circle back to where it came from – it crashed into the harbour wall and I got swept away up the river, 'cos the tide was coming in by that time. Then I was fished out by Jeremy, the man who called you. While he was out, Grote, who was living next door with Mouseman, came to ask about something, saw me and captured me again. That's the whole story, Jack,' I finished, breathlessly.

Phil turned his big, broad face around and stared at me directly with those hard, hazel eyes of his.

'I don't believe a word of it,' he said.

'Oh yeah?' I said. 'Why not?'

'Because you're not worth six cabbages and a chicken. I wouldn't give a half-eaten pizza for you.'

'You kerk!' I yelled.

Jack said, 'Hey, that's enough. You don't call my partner names, all right? He's kidding you. Don't you know when you're being kidded?'

'I wasn't kidding,' said Phil, his shirt all screwed up around the collar and his tie askew where he had turned around, 'I wouldn't give a rotten apple for these two.'

When we got to the station house, Jack went off to get John Woo released from the holding cells. Phil took us through the room where the detectives sat at their desks, interviewing witnesses and criminals alike. You could tell the difference between them. Those suspected of a crime were handcuffed to a bolt sticking out from the heavy desk. There were all sorts of people there, from kids to old grannies. I glanced at one or two of them as we passed. Some looked angry, some looked scared, some looked plainly bewildered.

Then, as we passed one desk, where a detective was interviewing a witness without handcuffs, I recognized a face.

'Largo!' I cried.

The man from the yacht looked up at me with a startled expression and then turned deliberately away, as if he didn't know me.

'Who?' asked Phil. 'What are you talking about, Hotwire?'

The other detective looked puzzled.

'I thought you said your name was Alex Janson,' he said to Largo. 'Why does this kid know you as someone else?'

'This man's a crook,' I said. 'He hangs around with a guy called Jake. They take stolen goods from the dockland thieves and sell them abroad. It was me who crashed their boat into the harbour wall.'

'Kid's got me confused with someone else,' said Largo, standing up. 'Well, thanks for your time, detective — I'll just waive the insurance on the yacht . . .'

He stood up, but Phil grabbed him from behind.

'Wait a second, *Mr Janson*. Let's talk this thing over. You came in here for a piece of paper to show your insurance company, right? Is that it, Pendle?' he asked the other detective.

'Yeah,' said Pendle. 'Said they had a malfunction on their steering computer and the yacht went into the harbour wall – but he needed our report on the incident to show the insurance company.'

Largo cried, 'You let me go – I got my rights. I came in here in good faith. You going to take the word of a street brat against mine? I'm an honest citizen.'

'Whenever someone says they're an honest citizen,' sighed Phil, 'I get awfully suspicious.'

They took Largo away and locked him up in the holding cell. I went through some screen shots of known criminals. Phil, the detective called Pendle, and the boss of the station house sat with me while I did it. Finally, after hundreds of unknown faces, the features of Jake filled the screen.

'That's him,' I said. 'That's Largo's partner. Only he's got a beard now. The captain of the yacht's not there though.'

'Maybe the captain's been clean until now,' grunted Phil. 'So, Hotwire, you can testify against these two slummers?'

I turned big round eyes on Phil.

'Yes, but Phil – you don't believe they bought me, do you? So none of this can be true. You said

103

I wasn't *worth* six cabbages and a chicken. You said . . .'

'Yeah, yeah,' snapped Phil, looking hot and uncomfortable under the gaze of his superior officer. 'You know I was kidding.'

Blindboy said sweetly, 'But Phil, you told us you *weren't* kidding. You said you didn't believe a *word* of what Hotwire was telling you. You said . . .'

'All right!' roared Phil. 'I – I apologize.'

His boss grinned at us and Pendle laughed. Jack came back then, accompanied by John Woo.

We had a big reunion, right there in the office.

'*Jo san*,' I said to John Woo. '*Nei ho ma*?'

'*M'ho*,' grumbled John Woo.

Jack told John Woo he was sorry the old man had been jailed.

'Mistakes will happen,' said John Woo, grudgingly. 'Now we have to decide what we can do about Mouseman.'

'Blindboy and me have got some bad news for you all,' I said, interrupting him. 'We've been saving this because it's pretty yerky stuff.'

'What is it?' asked Jack. 'Tell us, Hotwire.'

Blindboy said, 'Mouseman and Grote are going to bomb the city. He's going to hold the city to ransom. You'll be getting a message from him soon.'

Jack's superior officer said, 'How does he plan to do it – can we stop him?'

'Cybercats,' I said. 'He's going to convert all his

robber cybercats to bombs. Then he'll let them loose in the streets – a thousand cybercats with bombs in them. If you don't pay up, he'll set them off. One push of a button and they'll all be armed to go up at different times, in different places in the city. We won't stand a chance.

Phil cried, 'We'll shoot every stray cat in the city. We'll comb the streets and pull in all the rubbish-eating cybercats. Those left will be the cybercat-bombs. We'll get the bomb disposal squad to deal with them.'

Jack shook his head. 'That's knee-jerk reaction, Phil, and totally impractical. You don't tell us *how* we're going to get the cybercats to come in. Don't forget, they'll be programmed to avoid humans. We have to think of something more realistic. Let's just all go down to the canteen and bat this around for an hour or two. You don't need to be in on this, boss – I guess you'd better warn the mayor and corporation.'

'Thanks for telling me my duty, Sergeant Rickman,' said the boss, clearly peeved that he wasn't going to be in on the fun side of things. 'I shall enjoy telling the mayor this wonderful news – she's bound to be pleased with me.'

Jack looked shamefaced. 'Yeah, sorry it has to be you boss, but then – you *are* the boss.'

'Don't I know it,' said his superior officer, sighing.

We all went down to the canteen, where Jack

bought us drinks and buns. I scoured my brain for any idea which would help to stop Mouseman and Grote from destroying the city. John Woo came up with one or two suggestions. Phil Cannigan was still of the opinion that we ought to blast everything on four legs. Jack had no ideas at all – Jack's mind did not thrive on that kind of thought. He was not inventive.

Finally, Blindboy spoke. 'I've got it,' he said.

'What?' sneered Phil. 'Second sight?'

'That's not funny, Phil,' said Jack.

Phil said sorry and Blindboy explained.

'The thing is, we can't get near the cybercats because they're programmed to avoid humans, right? But real cats have natural enemies. One of those is dogs. What we do is, we make three packs of terrier dogs, programmed to recognize cybercats from real cats, and herd them one direction.'

'The kid's a genius,' cried Phil, willing to give credit where it was due. 'We could net the cybercats, take them away and blow them all up – rubbish-eaters and bombers together. That way we'd be sure to get them all.'

'Blow up our rubbish-eaters, smiff!' I grumbled.

'Phil's right,' said Jack. 'If we do it, we've got to be sure. We have to destroy all the cybercats.'

'Fair enough,' John Woo said. 'Now, Hotwire, Blindboy and myself had better go back to the Golden Arcade. We have work to do. We have a cyberdog to design . . .'

9

John Woo, Blindboy and me got to work on the blueprints for the cyberdog that very night. By the time morning came, we had some plans on the computer, ready to be copied. Blindboy even managed to get a 'bark' into the program, to make the dogs more authentic. They would yap like real dogs.

We got everyone working on the mass production of the cyberdogs straightaway. There wasn't a great deal of time. Mouseman had said that the fourth of July was the day something was going to happen. I guessed that was the day the first bomb would be exploded. It was nearing the end of June. We only had a few days.

I went along to the false fur company and asked for something that looked like dog pelts.

'Dog?' said the guy. 'Who the smiff wants to wear dog fur?'

'Well, dogs do for a starter,' I said, not wanting him to become suspicious about our plans for a cyberdog, 'and you'd be surprised how many people out there on the street think that dog hair is really swazz.'

The man raised his eyebrows. 'Yeah? You mean there's a kind of cult dog following?'

'Something like that. You remember when plastic supermarket bags were swazz street gear? Well, they're drummo now. Dog fur is in – every creaser on the street wants to be seen in dog fur. I've got a big order for you here . . .'

He stared at the order form I had filled in and his eyes widened.

'Who'd have thought it,' he said. 'One week it's cat fur, the next, dog. Amazing. Look, I'll have to make this batch up for you – we don't keep any lookalike dog fur in stock. You come back in two days and we'll fill the order.'

'Great,' I said. 'See you in two days.'

In the meantime our technicians, mostly the kids from the dumps, were working like crazy. We chose to make the terriers pretty small, so that they didn't take up a great deal of material. They weren't much bigger than the cybercats in fact. But we programmed the herding instinct into them, so that they would descend on the cybercats in packs of twenty, and drive the electro-mechanical creatures into steel nets in the way that sheep dogs round up their woolly charges.

Jack Rickman asked us one day, 'How do the dogs know what to chase? I mean, why don't they chase *real* cats? Or skidders? Or toy mice?'

'There's one component in the cybercat which is our own invention,' I explained to him. 'It's a microchip we manufactured ourselves. It's not in any other electronic device in the city – and it stands to reason it's not in a live cat.'

'You sure about that – that it's not in some other device – a fridge, or a microwave oven?'

'No,' John Woo confirmed. 'Hotwire made it herself.'

'OK,' he granted me. 'You've got a unique chip – what are you going to do with it?'

I grinned and showed him a miniature model skidder worked by remote radio control. It was about the size of my fist.

'I've put the cybercat microchip in this.'

I put the model skidder on the shop floor, then walked away from it. When I was a good two hundred metres away down the Golden Arcade corridor with Jack and the others, I told Blindboy to release three cyberdogs.

The dogs just wandered around our feet at first, as if they were sniffing the air. Then I switched on the model skidder and sent it zipping along the corridor. The cyberdogs immediately sprang to life and began barking and chasing the skidder as it nipped in and out of shop doorways.

Since it was early in the morning there were no shoppers and most of the other shop owners were still lying asleep. I steered the tiny skidder under their beds, through their belongings, around pillars, by waste bins. The dogs went charging after it, barking and yapping, copying its skidding

109

turns, waking everyone in the building. I knew I would not be very popular afterwards, but the test was important to us.

'They're going to get the skidder!' yelled Jack, excitedly.

At that moment, just before the lead dog pounced, I switched off the miniature skidder using the remote control.

The cyberdogs all slid to a halt, looking confused, and began wandering around sniffing the air again.

'How come?' Jack said. 'Why don't they get it?'

'Because I've switched off the microchip,' I said. 'It's just a piece of plastic and metal now. It's not a live component. The chip is only different from every other component when it's switched on and working live.'

'I'll take your word for it,' smiled Jack.

The whole operation had to be a closely kept secret, because if Mouseman got to hear of it, he would probably explode his cybercat-bombs early.

It was good to have Jack Rickman back with us and he took us all out, including John Woo, for a Vietnamese meal. Barb met us at the restaurant. Actually, it was more of a street cafe under a ragged awning than a restaurant, but that was fine because Blindboy and me weren't exactly dressed for one of those swazz places where the waiters hold their heads as if they're carrying a drip on the end of their nose.

Barb arrived at the restaurant breathless. She'd come straight from duty at the hospital, she said. Barb was dressed in a smart grey suit, with a tight skirt and fitted jacket. She looked swazz as usual. I wanted to be just like her when I grew up. She always looked attractive, even after a race across town. And she was so brainy it made your head spin.

If she was a politician, I would have voted for her straightaway – if I could vote, which I can't, because I'm too young.

Under Barb's arm was a brown paper parcel. I hoped it was presents for Blindboy and me. She often did that – brought us things. Blindboy heard the rustle of the parcel and kicked me under the table. He guessed I'd be staring and wanted to warn me about being rude and bad mannered and that sort of stuff. I looked down quickly and carefully inspected my knife and fork, pretending I hadn't been gawping at the parcel.

Blindboy didn't like the idea of people thinking we had dump manners. He always said I had no social graces. Blindboy is usually right about those things.

Barb said to me, 'Hotwire, I've brought you a dress, from one of my sister's girls. It's in good condition.'

I looked up, disappointed, and wrinkled my nose. 'What colour is it?'

'Party pink,' said Barb, and while my heart was

sinking, she added for good measure, 'with white lace trimming.'

'Aw . . .' I said, and got another kick from Blindboy under the table, so I lied, 'That's very nice, Barb. Thank you so much. I – I've always wanted a pink dress.'

I swallowed quickly, before I was sick.

Jack laughed out loud.

'What's the matter?' I asked him, angry.

'You tell the biggest untruths I've ever heard,' laughed Jack, 'and not very well, either.'

Barb smiled and said, 'I was just teasing you, Hotwire. It's a pair of jeans. There's a pair for Blindboy too. They're the latest colour – green stonewash.'

'Swazz!' I yelled, grabbing the parcel.

'Manners!' cried Blindboy.

'Yea,' I said, more quietly. 'Thanks, Barb. Thanks a big lot, from me and Blindboy.'

'I can thank her myself – I've got a tongue,' said Blindboy. He took his jeans from me and felt them. 'Thanks, Barb.'

'You're welcome,' she said, smiling. 'Both of you.'

John Woo said, 'They're good children. They help me a lot at the shop.'

I explained to Barb. 'John Woo is our grandfather now, aren't you, John Woo?'

'Sort of,' he smiled at Barb. 'But it looks like being a full-time job.'

Jack said, 'Let's order. Who wants lemon crab claws? How about some egg fried rice? Who likes prawns?'

We all ordered and had a good meal. It was really swazz having John Woo, Jack and Barb, and Blindboy and me all around the same table. It was like my whole family was with me. I wanted that meal to last for ever.

Later we all went back to the workshops.

It was murky and gloomy in the Golden Arcade at night. Some of the owners or assistants slept on rattan beds inside or outside their shops, but they used only small wattage bulbs to save on electricity.

There were little islands of yellow light along the dim, dark corridors.

We found our shop and showed Barb and Jack the cyberdog we had made – the terrier.

'Looks real enough,' said Barb. 'Just like a flesh-and-blood dog.' She stroked it. 'The coat feels real.'

'Synthetic Fur Company,' I said. 'We wouldn't use real fur for them.'

Barb smiled. 'No, of course you wouldn't. How many have you got now?'

John Woo said, 'Enough to make a few packs. It's the third of July tomorrow – we have to round up the cybercats before Mouseman begins letting off his bombs on the fourth.'

'It's a big operation,' I told Barb.

At that moment I saw a shadow detach itself

from the wall not far from where we were standing. It moved quickly along the corridor, between the rows of shops with their open fronts. I recognized the shape at once.

'Jack!' I yelled. 'Grote was listening!'

At my shout the figure of Grote began running, heading towards the broken-down escalator. Jack took off after him and I was close behind. Grote almost threw himself down the escalator stairs, with Jack right on his heels.

I slid down the escalator banister grip and landed in a heap in a pile of cardboard boxes left there by the shop owners. A cybercat which had been quietly munching on wet vegie cardboard, took off like a rocket, out through the market gateway and into the night streets.

By the time I'd picked myself up and made my way outside, Jack was standing there looking frustrated.

'He had a skidder waiting for him,' said Jack. 'Went up to snoop around, no doubt – then we came back.'

'Mouseman will know what we're up to now,' I cried.

'Then we'll have to get busy tonight,' said Jack, taking out a portable phone.

Jack called his headquarters and put out an alert on Mouseman's skidder. At the same time he asked for assistance in setting up the steel nets on some wasteland outside the city. It was to this place our dogs were programmed to drive the cats. Then we went back to the others.

'Mobilize,' said Jack. 'Get your cyberdogs into operation.'

He explained to John Woo what had happened.

John Woo went along the corridor, crying, 'Up! Everybody up!' and rousing the other shop and stall owners.

We gathered together the dogs, who shuffled and twitched, standing in their hundreds.

'You ready, Blindboy?' I asked my pal.

'You betcha!' said Blindboy.

Outside the market building the cyberdogs split automatically into packs and ran off yelping down streets and alleys. Phil arrived in a police bender. Jack, Blindboy and me piled into this vehicle, while Barb and John Woo went into another. We took off, cruising the streets.

Our cyberdogs did a good job of rounding up the cybercats, herding them out towards the city's edge. There, on the stretch of wasteland, was a third of the police force, waiting with steel nets hung from strong poles. Into these nets, as planned, the cybercats were driven, screeching and yelling for all they were worth. Fur was flying in all directions as some cats – maybe real ones – turned to fight the terriers. It was an asthmatic kid's worst nightmare, with the air full of dust and hair.

It was also pandemonium, what with packs of

dogs running through the streets of the city, and wailing cats being driven before them. The street people didn't know what had hit them. Those sleeping on the ground in doorways or under bridges were trampled on by cats and dogs alike. Luckily the animals, both real and computerized, were mostly light in weight. The street people started whacking out with rolled up newspapers and shoes, trying to get their own back on the stampeding animals.

Then there was the problem of *real* dogs, who joyously joined on to the packs of cyberdogs, probably thinking there was a revolution and dogs were going to rule the world. These often larger animals – German Shepherds, Golden Retrievers, Doberman Pinschers and even one female St Bernard – were bowling over citizens of the city who had come out of their houses to investigate the cause of the commotion.

Then there were the *real* cats, who were much more aggressive than the computerized ones. They turned on the dogs, spitting and hissing, their fur standing on end in a fearsome way. These feral cats were inclined to leap on the cyberdogs and tear the fur from their backs, exposing the machinery underneath. Around the city there were trails of nuts and bolts, pieces of computer, wires and bulbs, all littering the pavements and roads where a cyberdog was slowly unravelling itself in flight.

Out on the wasteland, where noise, flesh, plastic and metal were all coming together, caught in steel nets, the media had begun gathering. They had their spies out in the streets. There were freelance TV squads roaming the city, watching and waiting for unusual incidents.

These freelance TV squads had cameras mounted on jeeps, ready to video anything and everything. Normally it was some madman who had gone berserk with a weapon, or gangland fights, but here tonight they were able to film what must have seemed to them to be the end of the world. Noah's Ark had been opened and the animals let loose amongst the urban population.

'What's happening, Jack?' cried one news reporter, above the cacophony. 'What's going on?'

We all climbed out of the bender, while Jack was saying, 'These cats and dogs have been a nuisance in our streets for too long now – the police department are doing something about it.'

The reporter looked disgusted. 'Aw, come on, Jack – you don't expect me to believe you're just cleaning up the feral problem? Since when has the whole police force mobilized itself in the middle of the night to catch a few strays? There's more to it than that – I'm not a drummo, Jack.'

'Well, that's the official line,' said Jack, seeming to sympathize with the reporter a little. 'Stick around – you may learn more later.'

Just at that moment the bomb disposal people

117

arrived with a fanfare of horns and a blaze of lights. There were ambulances directly behind these vehicles. The police began to widen the circle around the nets full of captured cybercats. A screen was put up to the utter disgust of the TV reporters. Then they seemed to realize it wasn't just a barrier to prevent them from seeing what was occurring. It was *more* than that.

One of them shouted, 'Hey, isn't that a *bomb* screen? What's going on behind there? Is there a danger of explosion? What the smiff is happening here?'

'Just keep back,' yelled the police. 'Give the officers some room . . .'

The bomb squads got to work quickly. The bombs themselves were rather crude in construction, even though they were inside sophisticated equipment. There were no trembler devices or other safeguards to prevent the bomb disposal officers from dismantling them. Mouseman had been in too much of a hurry to worry about little details like that.

Consequently, it was just a case of grabbing a cybercat and snipping a couple of wires before its claws ripped through the thick gloves the officers wore to protect their hands.

By midnight, it seemed that all the cybercats had been disarmed. The protective screens were taken down. The real cats and dogs, looking very disgruntled, were allowed to go free. Most of the cats raced or slunk away over the wasteland, eager to be out of contact with these meddling humans.

A woozy feeling came over me during the evening, gradually creeping through my body, making me weak.

'I don't feel so good,' I said to Blindboy. 'I think that river water's caught up with me.'

He came over to me and placed a hand on my forehead.

'You're all hot,' he said. 'Maybe you should go and lie down somewhere?'

'Nah, I want to see this finished,' I said. 'I'll hold on for a bit longer.'

'OK, but be careful,' said my friend.

The real dogs were strolling or sauntering away now, looking huffy and proud. The canine revolution was now in tatters, but they weren't going to show that they cared about this. They were noble beasts of the streets, the hounds of the city, and they weren't going to run or droop like the cats.

The media got busy, telling the people of the city over the TV or radio, that a plot to blow them up in their beds had been foiled, and that two kids were involved. That was us. John Woo made sure we got some publicity. It wouldn't do any harm to our business for people to know we were swazz at computers.

Blindboy and me noticed some of our cyber-dogs, on the far side of the wasteland.

'Let's go and pick them up,' I suggested. 'We could recycle the parts, now we don't need them.'

'You go get them,' said Blindboy. 'I want to stay here to listen to the reporters.'

'All right.'

I set off, onto a lonely patch of ground where the shadows of people caught in bright lights were darting back and forth. They were like phantoms flitting here and there, as the police and media lamps were dismantled. It was kind of eerie out here, where the cyberdogs were roaming.

Over the past hour the feeling of sickness that had been creeping over me was getting worse. I realized, as I walked along, that I wasn't well. My head was spinning and I felt a bit queasy in my stomach. I tried to shake it off, by taking deep breaths of night air.

At that moment police sirens could be heard pursuing a suspect through the streets. I knew who they were chasing. As if to confirm my thoughts a skidder came hurtling out of the night's darkness onto the wasteland, churning up dirt.

Through the windscreen of the skidder I could see the hunched form of Mouseman, his mouth snarling, as he bent over the controls of the skidder, which lurched to a halt.

'It's Mouseman,' I shouted, back to Blindboy. 'He's come to get us!'

10

Grote leapt from the skidder, grabbed me, and hustled me into the back of the vehicle. I saw Blindboy running towards the sound of the skidder, calling for help. Mouseman began to drive the skidder towards Blindboy. He was going to run him down. He was going to kill Blindboy.

'No, you don't,' I yelled, and started clawing his neck with my nails.

'Get her off me,' shrieked Mouseman.

He lost control of the skidder for a moment and we plunged into the darkness, missing Blindboy by a fraction. Grote ripped me away from Mouseman. He pressed me into my seat and locked me there with the metal-armed seat belts.

'You stay put,' growled Grote.

Then to Mouseman, he said, 'You hurt, boss?'

'Of course I'm hurt,' snarled Mouseman, regaining control of the vehicle. 'The brat tore into my neck. She's like a wildcat, that one. Keep her away from me. I've got to concentrate. We have to throw them off our trail. There's a dozen police benders behind.'

I looked up into the rear view mirror above

Mouseman's head and could see the police benders following, their lights flashing but their sirens silent. A cat dashed across the headlights behind us. It had been hiding in an empty oil drum. It must have been the last cat on the whole landscape, live or robotic. It looked like an ordinary feral cat, the way it moved.

'Is that one of ours?' Mouseman asked Grote.

'They all look the same to me,' said Grote. 'They all look like ordinary cats.'

'They're supposed to,' snarled Mouseman, stopping the skidder. 'I just thought you knew.'

The cat was now directly between us and the cop benders.

Mouseman took a small, handsized device out of his pocket and pressed a button. There was a terrific explosion behind us and bits of fur, metal and plastic – along with a ton of dirt – rained down on the roof of the skidder. The cybercat had blown itself to smithereens. Mouseman turned white.

'Did you see that? Smiff! If only we still had the other cat bombs – I could rule this city.'

There was a deep, smoking crater behind us, where the cybercat-bomb had stood. It really had been a powerful blast. My ears were still ringing and my throat felt dry.

The hole didn't stop the police benders for long, however. Once they had recovered from their shock, they began to drive around the blasted area. Mouseman took off again.

Mouseman's skidder was a fast vehicle, faster than any police bender. He got a good distance ahead, until the lead police bender was behind a corner. Then he slipped smartly into a narrow alley and switched off the skidder's engine.

'We'll hide here,' he said, 'until they've all gone past.'

Unfortunately for me, his plan worked, and the police benders all drifted past the end of the alley, chasing a nonexistent prey.

I was seriously scared now. If Mouseman was prepared to run down a blind boy, he certainly wasn't going to worry about murdering the girl who had messed up all his plans. I imagined all sorts of horrible deaths. I'm good at thinking in pictures like that. They say cowards die many times. You don't have to be a coward to do that, you just have to be like me and have a good imagination.

I was also feeling more poorly by the minute. I could see my face in Mouseman's rear view mirror and I looked a pasty grey. My stomach was churning over.

'Let me go,' I said. 'It'll be worse for you when they catch you, if you hurt me.'

Mouseman turned and glared at me. I could see the hate in his eyes. If he could have killed me there and then, he would have done so. However, the reason he did not do away with me at that moment became obvious with his next words.

'I need you – if we come across any roadblocks.'

I knew what he meant. I was his hostage. He would promise the authorities to let me live, if they allowed him free passage through any roadblocks. I seriously wondered whether the police authorities would care about what happened to an ex-dump kid. They weren't all Jack Rickmans. It seemed to me they wouldn't care less what happened to me, if it meant recapturing a master criminal.

I didn't say this to Mouseman, in case he believed me and decided I wasn't worth anything after all.

'OK,' I said. 'If you like, I'll negotiate for you – at the roadblocks.'

'You'll keep your mouth shut,' warned Mouseman. 'I know you and your tricks. Grote, see she stays mum. Break her neck if she so much as utters a word.'

Grote's big head, seated directly on thick, heavy shoulders with serious ski slopes, nodded sombrely. Tiny eyes like those of a small, vacant-headed bird glittered at me from his big-boned face. There was no intelligence behind those eyes, but he understood this instruction. Grote might not understand many words in English, or in any other language, but straight commands to commit violent acts were well within his grasp.

'You touch me and you'll be in bad trouble,' I warned him. 'There's a law against hurting kids.'

Immediately, Grote looked confused.

Mouseman stared at us in the rear view mirror and shook his head disgustedly. 'Don't listen to that drivel, Grote. Just do as you're told, understand?'

Grote nodded again, glad to be told what to think.

'Anyway,' I said, swallowing hard to stop myself from gagging. 'I feel sick.'

Mouseman sneered at me. 'Yeah, yeah – I seem to have heard that somewhere before. Tell it to the birds, kid.'

At that moment I threw up all over the back of his seat: hot steaming vomit that smelled awful.

Mouseman looked horrified. 'Aw, smiff!' He looked into my face. 'The kid is *really* ill. Clean up that mess, Grote.'

Grote took out a box of tissues and began mopping up my vomit. He looked a bit ill himself. I moved to the far side of the skidder. I was feeling quite giddy and I had a headache. Mouseman opened all the windows and released some fragrance from a perfumed air freshener he had in the glove compartment.

'*Stinks* in here,' he said. 'Girl, if I thought you'd done that on purpose . . .'

'Sure,' I gasped, still heaving on a dry stomach, 'I – love – being – ill.'

Mouseman pulled out into the lonely back streets again, dark and gloomy now the police skidders had gone. Once we were on the highways and in the mainstream of traffic, Mouseman stood a good chance of escaping notice.

Somehow I had to attract attention to his skidder.

The wind was rushing in and clearing the smell a bit. I thought about leaning out of the window and yelling, but I knew that would be a short-lived exercise. Grote would be quite happy for an excuse to break my neck for me.

Then I remembered what I had in my pockets!

In the right hand pocket of my new jeans I had the miniature skidder we had used to test the cyberdogs. In my left pocket was the remote control device. As we cruised along, still in the dark back streets, I switched on the remote. The model skidder was now live and humming quietly to itself, though not so loud that the other two could hear it.

In a little while dogs began to appear, small terriers, racing behind us. They came out of the alleys and side streets, swerving after Mouseman's skidder. A determined bunch, they had the power to keep up with our vehicle, sprinting alongside us, occasionally snapping at the back of the skidder.

'What the . . .?' said my witless guardian, searching for a very difficult word in his tiny mind.

'Smiff?' I offered him.

Mouseman glared into the rear view mirror and a frown appeared on his forehead.

'What's going on?' he cried, as more and more dogs appeared. Soon we had all three packs of cyberhounds, racing after the skidder, barking and yapping.

A patrolman on a motorzip went by going the other way. He saw the dogs, some of them now leaping up onto the bonnet of the skidder, and back down again. His head swivelled and he did a U-turn on his motorzip, following us. A siren started wailing from his motorzip and I could see him barking into the microphone inside his helmet, presumably calling for back-up.

'We're being followed, boss,' said Grote.

'Very quick, Grote,' I said. 'Only forty dogs and a cop on a motorzip.'

Mouseman cursed and turned quickly down a slip road which led to the deserted dockland area.

'We'll get rid of the dogs here,' he snarled, 'and throw off that yerky motorzip moron as well.'

It was foggy down by the river and difficult to see more than a few metres ahead. We had to slow down and cruise carefully, Mouseman's vision being impaired. Once or twice we struck an object a glancing blow, making Mouseman curse.

On the river itself, boat foghorns were moaning, muted by the thick mist that swirled up from the cool water. They sounded like lost zombies might sound, looking for their graves. It was a forlorn, hopeless groan of a dull-minded creature whose brain had the quickness and brightness of lead.

'Some of your friends out there, Grote,' I said.

He looked at me in a bewildered way, before staring out of the window, trying to see what I was talking about.

We weaved in and out of rusting cranes, old ship's buoys, anchors and chains, and all the other paraphernalia I'd found on the dockside when I visited earlier. Finally we came to the remains of a bridge which had once spanned two quays. The middle section was missing. Between was a stretch of water.

'Hang on, Grote,' said Mouseman, revving the engine. 'We're going to jump it.'

We shot forward, the dogs still milling round us, yapping like crazy.

I held my breath as we went up the first part of the bridge and used it like a ramp, then went sailing over the gap between the quays. I looked out of the window and felt sick as I saw green, stagnant water flashing past us underneath. We hit the other side on a hard cushion of air and slewed sideways. Mouseman stopped the skidder.

The dogs kept coming – plop, plop, plop – one after another they fell into the water and sank. They were like lemmings intent on committing suicide. The gap over the water was too far for them to leap, yet they were magnetically drawn to the chip in the model skidder I had in my pocket.

I switched off the remote and the dogs stopped throwing themselves over the edge of the quay.

'Hey,' said Mouseman, puzzled, 'those dogs aren't swimming – they're going down like stones.'

I realized he still knew nothing about the cyber-dogs.

'Must be heavy dogs,' I murmured.

He looked back at me sharply, but by that time the motorzip cop had appeared on the other side of the quay. I could see by the way he was manoeuvring his machine he was not prepared to jump the gap. I didn't blame him. He probably didn't have the power in his machine to fly through the air like we had done. In the end he rode off, travelling along the edge of the quay, no doubt searching for a way around it.

'Right,' said Mouseman, 'let's go.'

He was about to pull away in the skidder, when strange figures appeared out of the darkness and mist around us, preventing him from driving off.

Mouseman must have been startled, because I saw him jump when they moved into the swirling fog lit up by his headlights. They were like wraiths which seemed to have formed out of the black evening hours: lean, hungry-looking spectres, out searching for victims. The vapours of the night clung to them like drifting veils, changing their shapes constantly. It was as if they were made of mist themselves. Then their eyes shone in the

129

brilliance of the skidder's lights, and their white and black faces appeared before us.

'Turn off them damn lights,' said a wasted-sounding voice.

Mouseman did as he was asked, instinctively, I think, having been badly frightened by the supernatural way these creatures had materialized out of the darkness and fog.

'Get out of the way,' yelled Mouseman nervously, out of the window. 'Who are you? What do you want?'

'You have to pay the toll,' said a thin man. 'You have to pay us a fee for going through our property.'

It was then that we realized they were ordinary human beings, just like us.

Despite my illness, I grinned. It was Dave and his crowd of dockland thieves. There were so many of them around the skidder Mouseman couldn't possibly drive through them, even if he didn't care who he hit. More and more came out of the derelict warehouses and huts around the site. Mouseman was trapped inside a ghostly mob of ragged outlaws.

Grote got out of the car and, magically, iron bars appeared in the hands of the men and women surrounding our vehicle. Grote snatched one of the iron bars and bent it slowly and purposefully before their eyes until it was a loop. He hung it around the owner's neck, like a garland. The bar was three centimetres thick. Many docklanders were impressed by this display of strength, taking a step back, but Dave stood his ground.

'You must pay the toll,' insisted Dave. 'You have to pay us for being on our property.'

'*Your* property?' roared Mouseman, not intimidated any longer. 'This is *government* property.'

Dave smiled, grimly. 'Do you see any government people here? The government left this place years ago. It's rusting to bits. It's *our* property now, by squatters' rights. The government abandoned it – to us.'

'If you don't get out of the way,' cried Mouseman, frantically, 'I'll drive through the lot of you . . .'

At that moment the night caterwauled. The sound of sirens filled the air all around us. Dave and his army of ghosts disappeared, magically, before our eyes. They vanished like shreds of mist into their hidey-holes.

Mouseman had waited too long. Now we were surrounded by police benders, all training their headlamps on us. Our vehicle was caught like an island in a sea of bright light. Mouseman screamed and thumped the dashboard in his anger. First the outlaws had encircled us, now we were ringed by the law itself.

Grote, the poor fool, tried to run.

Mouseman shouted after him, 'Come back here, you stupid idiot – you can't get away like that.'

But it was too late. Policemen and policewomen leapt on Grote like terriers on a bear. There was a tremendous struggle, with people in blue uniforms flying across the ground, only to pick themselves up again and to dive back into the scrimmage. Finally, the mighty Grote was subdued, his wrists cuffed, and he was led shambling away like a defeated giant.

The police began to close in on Mouseman's skidder.

Mouseman pulled a stubby gun from one of his pockets. The stocky little man turned and placed the muzzle of the gun against my forehead. Sweat was pouring from his brow. He looked almost as feverish as I felt. I heard the click of the hammer as he cocked the weapon. He yelled at the approaching cops.

'Come any closer and I'll blow the kid's brains out!'

The advancing line of blue uniforms stopped in its tracks.

11

'Don't do anything stupid, Mouseman,' yelled a voice I recognized as that of Jack Rickman. 'You can't get away – you're surrounded. Give yourself up.'

'Give yourself a kick in the head,' retaliated Mouseman with a snarl. 'I swear I'll kill the kid if you come any closer. I want safe passage out of here.'

I looked into Mouseman's frenzied eyes and knew he would do as he said. His gun hand was trembling violently and the trigger was wet with his perspiration. I was sick and dizzy from my illness, but I was still frightened enough to call out.

'Jack, don't come any closer. He means it.'

'OK, Hotwire – don't worry,' called Jack. 'We'll get you out of this. How are you feeling?'

'Sick,' I said. 'I'm ill.'

Mouseman yelled, 'Enough of this gabbing – get those cops out of the way. I'm driving through.'

There was silence now. It was a standoff. Then at an order from Jack the cops shuffled backwards, until they were about a hundred metres away from the skidder.

Still they did not part ranks.

While the line of police faced the vehicle and Mouseman's trembling hand held the gun to my head, a cat strolled out of the swirling edge of darkness and jumped up onto the bonnet of our skidder. It licked its paws, then settled there, quietly, curling up in the way that cats do, with its tail draped around it and its head resting on its front paws.

A policeman's voice drifted over the empty space to us. 'Where the smiff did that cat come from?'

At that moment, Blindboy stepped through the line of policemen. He spoke to the cop who had shouted, then came forward about fifty metres. He confronted Mouseman's skidder like a small colossus, his legs apart and his shoulders squared. He seemed to be blocking our way.

'Get out of here, Blindboy,' I yelled. 'He'll drive over you.'

'You better believe it!' shouted Mouseman.

Blindboy put his right hand in his pocket.

'OK, you kerk,' called Blindboy. 'Let's see if you like a taste of your own medicine. John Woo and me made some cybercat bombs of our own, just in case. That's what you have there on the bonnet of your skidder. I'm going to detonate it and blow you to pieces, you slummer. I've got a remote control device in my pocket. My finger's on the button right now. How does that sound to you?'

Mouseman looked at the cat, then at Blindboy, and then at me. He took the gun away from my temple.

'That's not a cybercat,' he said, his voice full of confidence. 'That's a mangy old feral cat.'

'You'd like to believe that, wouldn't you?' laughed Blindboy. 'You'd really like to believe that. I'm going to count to ten, then press the button. Goodbye, Hotwire – see you in the other place, when I get there.'

I didn't know what Blindboy was playing at, but I knew he wouldn't blow me up. At least, I thought I knew. Maybe he was so mad at Mouseman he would do anything? Maybe he thought I'd stand a better chance with a bomb than I would with Mouseman? Maybe he *was* going to blow up the skidder.

Mouseman sniggered. 'You expect me to believe you'd blow *her* up too? Just to get me? Go to blazes.'

'Ah, well,' said Blindboy, cocking his head to one side, 'there's the thing, Mouseman. You see, Hotwire caught a deadly disease when she fell into the river. She's going to die in any case, so it seems a good way to put her out of her misery. She knows that modern medicine can't save her. That's why she's so reckless. She doesn't care any more.'

Mouseman was sweating again. 'Hey,' he laughed, a little hysterically, 'that's a lot of rubbish talk. Hotwire isn't dying of anything . . .'

He turned to stare at me for a few moments and saw what I could see for myself in the rear view mirror: a ghastly, green-grey face, bloodshot eyes and shadowy sunken cheeks above a pale set of bloodless lips. I really *did* look as if I were dying. Maybe Blindboy knew something I didn't? Maybe there was an epidemic of cholera, or swamp fever, or typhoid, which Blindboy knew about, but not me? I didn't want to die in agony, like Blindboy had said. Best to go quickly.

'OK,' I called to Blindboy. 'I'm ready – press the button.'

'One – two – three – four – five . . .'

'You wouldn't do it,' screamed Mouseman, with a shudder. 'You *couldn't* do it. You couldn't kill people.'

'Listen, Mouseman, all my life people have been making fun of me because I'm blind. People like you. I just want to get my own back, that's all. Revenge. I hate you all. Six – seven – eight . . .'

'I don't believe you,' he shrieked. 'You're lying . . .'

'Nine— . . .'

'Wait, wait!' Mouseman threw the gun out of the skidder window and raised his hands. 'All right, I give in. Don't press that button. *Please* don't press that button.'

The police ran forward. One snatched the gun from the ground. Jack Rickman and Phil Cannigan wrenched open the door of the skidder and pulled

Mouseman out. Within a few moments the master criminal was handcuffed and being frogmarched towards the waiting police van. He dug in his heels.

'Wait a minute,' he cried, to the escorting cops. 'Just wait a minute.'

He looked back at Blindboy, then at the cat.

I said, 'He's looking at you, Blindboy. I think he wants to know if the cat is really a bomb.'

Blindboy smiled, felt his way to the car, and reached out and stroked the feral cat.

The animal arched its back, stretched and began purring.

'Flesh and blood,' called Blindboy. 'It jumped up there because it was warm, from the engine running. Don't you know anything about cats, Mouseman? You should do, with a name like you've got. You should know their habits.'

Blindboy turned his pockets inside out to show Mouseman he hadn't got a remote control device.

'Pity it's not April the first,' he said.

Mouseman snarled, 'One of these days . . .'

'But not today, kerk,' I yelled, making my head spin. I went over to Blindboy. 'Am I really that sick?' I asked.

Blindboy screwed up his face. 'Nah, 'course not. You've got 'flu, that's all. Jack says it's sweeping the whole neighbourhood. You'll be all right in a couple of days.'

I felt relieved.

137

John Woo, with Barb Rickman beside him, came over to us. 'You look very ill, Hotwire. We have to get you to bed.'

Barb said, 'She can come back with me – to our place.'

Jack Rickman, standing talking with Phil Cannigan, heard this and came striding over to us.

'Our place? She's got a good bed of her own.'

'Outside a *shop* in the Golden Arcade?' said Barb. 'Look, copper, I'm the doctor here. I say she needs proper treatment. Influenza can be very nasty if it's not taken seriously. You can sleep outside the shop, Jack.'

'Hey?' he said, looking pained. 'I'll sleep on the couch in our living room, if it's all the same to you, doc.'

He then turned and ruffled Blindboy's hair.

'Well done, pal. You did good. You can sleep at our place too, if you want. You get the armchair, OK?'

Blindboy grinned. 'OK, Jack.'

Blindboy combed his own hair with his fingers and smiled in my direction. Once again we had captured Mouseman between us. Blindboy had done most of the work this time, but I'd had to sit there dying of a fever with a gun to my forehead. I played my part in the drama too, even if I didn't actually *do* very much.

'Were you scared, Hotwire?' whispered Blindboy a little later, on our way to the Rickmans' in

Barb's bender. 'Did that gun on your temple scare you?'

'Who, me?' I snorted. 'Nah, 'course not. I *wanted* it there. It was like a cold compress, if you know what I mean? It was nice and cool, me being fever-ish and all that. I was *glad* he pressed the muzzle against my hot forehead.'

'You great liar, sure you were,' laughed Blind-boy. 'Sure you were. I could see you shaking in your shoes.'

'You could *see* me?' I said. 'Who's the great liar?'

'I could *feel* you. The whole world was shaking. You were like a big lump of jelly.'

'I was not. I was – *pretending* to be scared,' I said.

He laughed and punched me lightly on the arm, while Barb looked at us in the rear view mirror and smiled her motherly smile.

THE END

ABOUT THE AUTHOR

Garry Kilworth was born in York but, as the son of an Air Force family, was educated at more than twenty schools. He himself joined the RAF at the age of fifteen and was stationed all over the world, from Singapore to Cyprus, before leaving to continue his education and begin a career in business which also enabled him to travel widely.

He became a full-time writer when his two children left home and has written many novels for children and adults – mostly on science-fiction, fantasy and historical themes – including *The Drowners*, which was commended for the Carnegie Medal in 1992. He was the winner of the Gollancz/*Sunday Times* Short Story Competition in 1974, and of the 1992 World Fantasy Award. *The Electric Kid*, his first Transworld novel for young adults, won the Lancashire Libraries Children's Book Award in 1995.

He lives in a country cottage in Essex which has a large woodland garden teeming with wildlife, including foxes, doves, squirrels and grass snakes.

THE ELECTRIC KID

GARRY KILWORTH

'YOU JUST BROKE THE LAW. WE COULD TURN YOU OVER TO THE COPS TOMORROW, IF WE WANTED. YOU GOT TO COME AND WORK FOR US, OR YOU'LL END UP IN THE SWEATROOMS.'

Hotwire and Blindboy were a team. Sightless, Blindboy could home in on the electronic vibrations from junk buried in the dump where they lived. Hotwire could fix anything so that it worked again. It was neat. They made money. They could live.

But then Blindboy's special skills attracted the attention of Mouseman, the city's most feared criminal . . .

A dramatic and gripping thriller set in a decaying hi-tech future world.

'Has the ingredients of a successful story – interesting characters, lots of suspense, and an original plot'
                                                    THE SCHOOL LIBRARIAN

WINNER OF THE 1995 LANCASHIRE
CHILDREN'S BOOK AWARD

0 553 406566

A SELECTION OF TITLES AVAILABLE FROM BANTAM YOUNG ADULT BOOKS

THE PRICES SHOWN BELOW WERE CORRECT AT THE TIME OF GOING TO PRESS. HOWEVER TRANSWORLD PUBLISHERS RESERVE THE RIGHT TO SHOW NEW RETAIL PRICES ON COVERS WHICH MAY DIFFER FROM THOSE PREVIOUSLY ADVERTISED IN THE TEXT OR ELSEWHERE.